THE GREAT INTERACTIVE DREAM MACHINE

Novels for Young People by Richard Peck

Don't Look and It Won't Hurt
Dreamland Lake
Through a Brief Darkness
Representing Super Doll
The Ghost Belonged to Me
Are You in the House Alone?
Ghosts I Have Been
Father Figure
Secrets of the Shopping Mall
Close Enough to Touch
The Dreadful Future of Blossom Culp
Remembering the Good Times
Blossom Culp and the Sleep of Death
Princess Ashley
Those Summer Girls I Never Met
Voices After Midnight
Unfinished Portrait of Jessica
Bel-Air Bambi and the Mall Rats
The Last Safe Place on Earth
Lost in Cyberspace
The Great Interactive Dream Machine

THE GREAT INTERACTIVE DREAM MACHINE

Another Adventure in Cyberspace

Richard Peck

Dial Books for Young Readers

NEW YORK

Published by Dial Books for Young Readers
A Division of Penguin Books USA Inc.
375 Hudson Street
New York, New York 10014

Printed in the U.S.A.
First Edition

1   3   5   7   9   10   8   6   4   2

Library of Congress Cataloging in Publication Data
Peck, Richard, date
The great interactive dream machine: another adventure in cyberspace /
Richard Peck.—1st ed.
p.   cm.
Summary: Josh Lewis is unwillingly drawn into the computer experiments of
Aaron, his friend and fellow classmate at an exclusive New York
private school, and the two find themselves uncontrollably transported
through space and time.
ISBN 0-8037-1989-2
[1. Computers—Fiction.   2. Schools—Fiction.
3. Science fiction.]
I. Title.
PZ7.P338Gr   1996   [Fic]—dc20   95-53263   CIP   AC

To Madge and Bill Briggs,
and
Mei Li

1
Power Outage

My best friend used to be Aaron Zimmer.

Aaron's always been the shortest kid in class at Huckley School and the smartest. I've always been his best friend. Practically his only friend. We even get in the same trouble together, and we live in the same apartment building. I live on the twelfth floor. He lives up in the penthouse. We've been tight since preschool. You can ask anybody. But now in the spring of sixth grade, I don't see that much of him. When I do, his mind is somewhere else. He's mentally missing.

My mom says it's puberty. She says that when people hit puberty, they begin to go in different directions. Some of them go into orbit. This may explain Aaron. Basically he only relates to his computers. He spends so much time at his motherboard that he's forgetting how to interface with humans.

You get this with people who were given too much software at an early age. Call them vidkids. Some of them have logged so many screen hours with Gauntlet, SolarStriker, and PlayStation that they can't tell virtual reality from reality. Aaron may be an example of the worst-case scenario. If you X-rayed his skull, you'd probably see microchips and copper wiring. Just kidding, but I'm serious.

We're pretty different. Maybe too different. I like to read R. L. Stine. He likes to read *The Internet Yellow Pages*. In my dreams I'm falling from high places and seeing scary faces at windows. In Aaron's dreams he's probably surfing the Net and exploring Donkey Kong country. I like the weird and unexplained. Aaron *is* weird and unexplained.

Not everything we used to do was that much fun, but at least we did it together. Now on this spring Saturday I had zilch to do and nobody to do it with. Central Park was in full bloom. It was the perfect weekend, and it might as well be a school day. Why even get up?

I was up anyway, eating cold cereal. At the other end of the table was a letter in a Huckley School envelope. In my experience, any letter from a school to parents is bad news.

We try to be quiet on Saturday mornings because Miss Mather, the old lady who lives right below us on eleven, complains even if we're walking around in sock feet. She sends up little notes that say:

Stop jumping on my head.

Our apartment was beginning to stir. Mom was moving around in her room, and I heard whining. It was either Heather's hair dryer or Heather herself. Heather's my sister: seventh grade. I had a couple more minutes alone with my cereal, tops.

I'd brought a book to the table we had to read for Mr. Headbloom's class. It's *Time and Again* by Jack Finney, not a bad book considering that it isn't by R. L. Stine. Besides, there was going to be a quiz.

Mom came in.

On weekdays she dresses for success to go to her job at Barnes Ogleby. This morning she was in her Saturday gear: jeans, penny loafers, and her oldest college sweatshirt, the one with SAVE THE WHALES across the front. Mom's pretty even without makeup.

On her way to the coffee maker, she detoured to give me my morning hug. For a moment all I could see was SAVE THE WHALES. "Josh, summer's coming, and we have to talk."

If you're a kid anywhere else, summer's great. If you're a kid in New York, summer's just another problem.

"We really ought to call your dad." Mom tapped the letter from Huckley School. "We should get his feedback."

Dad's in public relations, working out in Chicago right now on the Lucky Mutt dog food account. My parents aren't exactly separated, but Mom says they get along better when they're in different time zones.

Then it happened.

The world went dim. The light over the table winked out. Every plug-in appliance went dead. The digital clock clicked once and went down. In the distance the whining stopped, so it was the hair dryer, not Heather.

Mom and I waited until Heather stumbled into the room looking like a damp dog. She was only about half blow-dried. "Mo-om," she said, "nothing *works.*" Being almost thirteen, Heather figured anything that went wrong was Mom's fault.

When the power goes, we look down from the front windows to see if the traffic lights are out. If they are, the whole city's shut down. This happens, and it's an excellent time not to be in the subway or trying to do ATM banking. Besides, it's interesting to see what happens to traffic without stoplights. Everybody stops. Then everybody goes at once. But the light down on Fifth and Seventy-second was operational. So it was probably just our building. This also happens.

Mom looked at me. "Aaron," she said.

I had to admit it was probably Aaron. His bedroom is so fully computerized that it could overload all the generators of a major nation.

Heather was making a turban out of her towel. "Typical," she sighed. "We ought to move to another building. I need more closets anyway."

While Mom went looking for a coffeepot that didn't plug in, I slipped out to check on Aaron. The apartment was pretty shadowy, so I wouldn't be missed for a minute.

Out of habit, I left through the front door. But it was

dark as a pocket out in the hall. Kicking sounds and swearing came from behind the elevator doors, so this was Vince the doorman. He'd probably been delivering the mail to our doors. From the sound of the swearing, Vince was trapped somewhere between our floor and eleven.

The only other way out is through the kitchen door and up the back stairs. As I crept past Mom, she said, "Josh, we really do need to talk."

"What about?" came Heather's voice behind me. "Is Josh in trouble at school again?"

By then I was out of there. When I'd climbed all the way up to the Zimmers' kitchen door, I was breathing hard. I pushed the bell. Habit again. I knocked, and the Zimmers' housekeeper opened up, holding a lighted candle. She doesn't speak much English, and she wasn't in that great a mood either.

"Aaron home?"

"And how," she said.

Behind her the oven door was open. She'd been taking out a half-baked cake that was never going to rise. The Zimmers have an all-electric kitchen.

Their place is a nice spread across the top of the building. About half the roof is their terrace, professionally planted, with top-of-the-line garden furniture. Their penthouse covers the other half. They have so many rooms that they don't run into each other very often. From the windows of their all-white living room you can see most of Manhattan.

I crept through it. Ophelia's usually on her silk cushion on the windowsill. She's a French poodle, white to color-coordinate with the room, and she's mainly Mrs. Zimmer's dog. When she sees me, she tends to bound over and try to take a chunk out of my ankle. Ophelia, I mean, not Mrs. Zimmer. So you always check to see where Ophelia is. She wasn't on her cushion. Her nose was sticking out from under a sofa. Something had scared her under the furniture, and I thought I knew what.

I followed the smell of a small electrical fire down a long hall to Aaron's room.

I pushed open his door. He's got a bed in there and a stack of *Byte* magazines from the school media center, and a book called *Navigating the Internet*. But the rest of the room is an ultra-high-tech, state-of-the-art, stand-alone microsystem workstation.

It's built around a pair of Big Blue's power PC's with a couple of high-definition TV screens and more add-ons and video assets than you can believe. We're talking mainframe here. It goes to the ceiling, with wires and cables snaking around the floor. Aaron calls it his personalized blendo-technopolis. He uses terms like this, and I don't know what they mean.

As late as last winter if Aaron wanted to mega-diddle his data on two keyboards at once, he had to use the computers in the school media center. We were both *this close* to getting in big trouble for being in there when we weren't supposed to be. Now I noticed that his home workstation had doubled in size.

Aaron's parents pretty much give him anything he

wants. But that's usually the way. Your best friend's parents give him more than your parents give you.

I didn't see Aaron. Needless to say, the lights were out. Steel-gray haze hung in the room. I looked all around. Then I checked behind the door, and there he was, crumpled in the corner. He's a funny-looking kid anyway. Very pale face. Bright-red hair going in every direction. Small feet. Small hands. Small all over. Today he looked like they'd started to electrocute him, but the governor called.

He has very baggy eyes for a kid, and they were really staring. He was holding a soldering iron in one hand. The fingers on the other hand were working away, punching up something in the air. He does that a lot, like he's working on a keyboard even when no keyboard's there.

"Aaron," I said, "if I touch you, will I fry?"

"You kidding?" he said. "The electricity's off."

I sighed. "And how did that happen? How did you manage to off the power in a sixteen-story building this time?"

"I'm thinking power surge." He began easing up the wall.

"Power surge? Does that soldering iron in your hand have anything to do with it?"

He looked surprised to find a soldering iron in his hand. But then he'd just been blasted out of his chair and across the room. Too bad it hadn't knocked some sense into him. "Oh well," he said, "back to the drawing board." Another one of his sayings.

"Tell me how it happened, Aaron. Talk me through it."

"You couldn't follow it."

"Try me."

We were standing in front of his technopolis. It was quiet, cooling. It was like some dead civilization. Aaron stroked his chin. "I was trying to go next generation with my equipment. Do you realize that the sixteen-bit Sega and Nintendo technology is already obsolescent now that game systems like 3DO and Atari have started processing data thirty-two or sixty-four bits at a time?"

"Hadn't heard," I said. "You about blacked out the Eastern Seaboard so you could play computer games?"

"I knew you wouldn't understand. Why try? That was just an example. You've got to keep upgrading. You've got to stay on the cutting edge." He stared up at me, and his eyes were little pink pinwheels. "Nothing is future-proof, Josh."

"Let's start farther back," I said. "You got up this morning. You went straight to your keyboards without combing your hair or brushing your teeth. You booted up your computers or whatever."

"I logged in. I had e-mail," Aaron said. "And that's another example. World Wide Web is to e-mail what television is to radio. We keep moving on. Today's technology is tomorrow's archaeology. Today you're happening. Tomorrow you're history."

"Fine," I said. "You had e-mail."

He nodded. "I join channels with a kid out in Hays, Kansas. Met him through a chat room."

"What's his name?"

"His user I.D. is Hayseed. His real name's Floyd."

Floyd?

"He was pretty excited today," Aaron said. "He'd just won his county's Jersey Cattle Club essay contest: 'Why I Would Like to Own a Jersey Calf.' He's heavy into 4-H."

I stared. "You're talking halfway across the country to a kid named Floyd who calls himself Hayseed and wants a cow? Aaron, that hurts. I live in your building. I'm right here."

He blinked up at me. "You don't have e-mail."

"Okay, forget Floyd. By the way, what's your user I.D.?"

"A2Z," Aaron said. At school we call him the A-to-Z man because he's named Aaron Zimmer and because he knows everything from A to Z. Thinks he does.

"What did you do next?"

His eyes got shifty. "I'm working on a new formula." The haze was lifting, and he glanced around the room. "I don't want to say too much about it. I don't want it to fall into the wrong hands."

"Don't worry about my hands," I said. "Just talk."

The only time we can talk these days is when his computers are down.

"Here's just an example," he mumbled. "In the next-generation stage we're looking at a holographic projector instead of a printer. Right? Transmission of three-D imagery, okay?"

"Hold it, Aaron. This is beginning to sound familiar." Because I remembered how he once got carried away with something he called "cellular reorganization." And I mean carried away. It meant being sent by your computer to other times. It meant that all the cells in your body reorganized and shipped out. I'm not saying it didn't work, but he never got the bugs out of the formula. I was hoping he was over it by now.

"It's not about cellular reorg—"

"That was an early stage."

"Where are we now?"

"Is it going to do me any good to recap fiber-optic potential for you?"

"Probably not." I looked at him. And I happened to notice his eyes were practically shifting off his face.

"F.L.I.R.," he said, almost whispering.

"F.L.I.R.?"

He threw out a small hand. "Shut up about it. We're talking a top-secret military device: *forward-looking infrared* system."

"I'll hate myself for asking, but if it's top-secret government stuff, how did you get it? E-mail?"

"Keep your voice down. I was hacking around at random and found myself in the Big P."

"Big P?"

"Pentagon," he breathed.

"Oh, right," I said. "Aaron, give me a break. You're a troll, but you're no mole."

But did he hear me? Forget about it. "What I needed was optimum programming for enough high-intensity three-dimensional image shifting that I could store here at home and digitize for any computer I happened to have access to. The Big P thinks F.L.I.R. is just a kind of post-radar for spotting triple A."

"Triple A?"

He sighed. "Anti-aircraft artillery."

"One of these days you're going to shoot yourself in the foot, Aaron. Just bottom-line me."

"I put together a formula, and the government helped. We're taxpayers, am I right? So then I found I could download imagery from the server at the rate of sixty pictures a second, enhanced by F.L.I.R." He patted a set-top box in his technopolis. "When I get this baby wired and running, I've got ten times the computing power of a top-of-the-line PC, with the added capacity for night fighting if we're interested. When you're downloading imagery from the server at the rate of sixty pictures a second, it can reorganize your total body and move it out. We could probably even bomb some other country if we had warheads. Theoretically."

"That's creepy, Aaron. So are you."

He shrugged.

"So to get enough computing power or whatever for your new formula to work, you started soldering live wires with the power on?" I said. "Is this what I'm hearing?"

"I'm under a lot of pressure," he said. "I'm looking at a deadline."

"What deadline? You mean like final exams?"

"Please," Aaron said. He doesn't set aside much time for schoolwork. "I'm working up a formula as a project for computer camp."

Computer camp?

"You're going to computer camp? This summer?"

"If I can get in," he said. "They don't want you in the advanced-digit-head division till you're twelve. I won't turn twelve till August, and I don't even look eleven. At our age we're not old enough for anything. But a really high-concept project might get me in. I need a project that will knock their socks off."

"And what's going to happen to me while you're knocking their socks off, Mr. High-I.Q. A-to-Z man? I can't go to computer camp. There's no way I could get in the gate."

"That's true." Aaron shook his head sadly. "You wouldn't know a modem from a mouse. You wouldn't know a megabyte from a microdisk. You wouldn't—"

"Okay, okay. So you know where I'll end up all summer."

Aaron nodded. "I'll end up there too if I don't take steps."

"Did your parents get the letter from the coach?"

He nodded again. "Can you believe he's still using U.S. post office snail mail in the age of the fax and e-mail?"

The parents of every kid at Huckley School got the same letter. It was from the middle-school coach, Trip Renwick. He was setting up a soccer camp in Connecticut, and he wanted everybody to sign on.

Soccer all summer? Fifty miles from the nearest bagel, bouncing balls off our heads? Vertically challenged Aaron and spindly me being pounded into a weedy field for two months? Living in bunks and listening to frogs? Please.

"It will look good to parents," Aaron said. "When

summer comes, they've got to do something with us. They're sitting ducks for a letter like that."

"Aaron, I'm depressed. Let's get some air."

"But as soon as the power comes on again, I can get back to—"

"Aaron. Think. You've blown the master fuse in a Fifth Avenue building. What about your parents? Where are they?"

"My dad goes into the office on Saturdays. My mom's at her aromatherapy class."

"Aaron, do you want to be around if they come home before the power's back on?"

"Not really," he said in a mouselike voice.

"Then let's go. It's called outdoors. You'd like it. We'll go across the park."

"We'll have to take Ophelia," he said. "The professional dog walker doesn't come on weekends. Weekends are for spending quality time with your pet."

"Aaron, let's not take Ophelia. Picture it. Two undersize private-school guys with preppy written all over us walking a white poodle with a rhinestone collar in Central Park? That's asking for trouble."

But at least he was willing to go. He reached for his small windbreaker. "Aaron, it's springtime. The sun's out. Forget the windbreaker."

As we were walking out of his room, a voice behind us spoke suddenly:

YOU HAVE E-MAIL

So the power was back on, but I got him out of there anyway.

2

Two Preppies and a Poodle

Ophelia was in a fairly good mood when she saw her imported Italian-leather leash. She showed me her teeth in the elevator, and she showed them to Vince down at the front door. But she didn't lunge. She was wearing her rhinestone collar. She'd been to the dog hairdresser. She was looking good and knew it.

We entered the park at Seventy-second past the T-shirt salespeople. The benches were full of oldsters holding up sun reflectors to their faces. There were runners, walkers, people on stilts. There were bikers in and out of the bike lane. The puppet-show people were performing. The gangsta-rap people were out, and the moonwalkers. You name it. There was enough of a crowd so nobody paid any attention to two preppies and a poodle.

We stayed away from the soccer field. Practically

every sunny school-day afternoon Coach Renwick marches us over to the park, dragging along the net goals with us. We pray for rain.

On our way to Bethesda Fountain, Aaron was nearly sliced and diced by a black-spandex flying wedge of Rollerbladers: big muscle monsters in Walkmans and earrings, with flying ponytails.

"Aaron, for Pete's sake, watch where you're going," I said. "They'll flatten you like Wile E. Coyote."

But you know Aaron. He was wandering along with Ophelia's leash in one hand and his other hand keyboarding like crazy.

People were sitting all around the fountain, eating frozen yogurt. The lake was full of boaters. Overhead the Fuji Film blimp was bobbing and weaving in a blue sky. One of the great New York views. Was Aaron seeing this? Was he enjoying a perfect spring Saturday?

"Look at it this way," he said. "You've got your basic NCSA Mosaic to point and click while you're browsing the Web, am I right?"

"Who knows?" I said. "Who cares?"

"Let's take that another interactive step."

"Let's not."

"The Internet as we know it—"

"Aaron, what are you saying? That you're about to come up with one of your cockamamie formulas again—that'll black out our building and send you to computer camp and leave me in droopy shorts up in Connecticut, running my legs off after a soccer ball? Is that what we're talking about?"

But Ophelia kept dragging at her leash, so we strolled

on. She did her business off the curb on Central Park West. Across the street was this big old building with towers and turrets. I like towers and turrets.

"Hey, Aaron, look. It's the Dakota apartment building."

Aaron snapped on a plastic glove and took a Baggie out of his jeans pocket. If you're going to walk a dog in New York, you're going to have to clean up after it. It's the law.

"So?" he said.

"The Dakota. It's where the novel *Time and Again* takes place."

"What novel?"

I sighed. "The novel Headbloom assigned us. The novel we're having a quiz on Tuesday."

"Ah," Aaron said. He signs himself out of a lot of classes to work on the computers in the media center. "You want to fill me in on that?"

"It's not a bad book for an assignment. It even has pictures," I said. "This guy named Si Morley goes back in time. It's a top-secret government project."

Aaron showed a little interest. He dropped the Baggie in a trash container. "How'd he do his time travel?"

"He did a lot of homework on the year 1882. He researched it."

Aaron nodded. "You can access that information on WAIS—Wide Area Information Servers. You can search information libraries stored on the Net."

"He didn't use that," I said. "He read books. Then he came over here to the Dakota, which was from the time he wanted to go to. He moved in. He wore old-fashioned clothes. He psyched himself back. It was like self-hypnosis."

"Fiction." Aaron sneered slightly.

"Of course it's fiction," I said. "But do you remember when you were first trying to cellular-reorganize yourself, you got into John D. Rockefeller's bed at the Museum of the City of New York? You thought that might send you back."

"I was a kid," Aaron said. "It was last winter."

"You said that really wanting to go is part of the deal. You called it—"

"Emotional Component," Aaron said. "Which is true, but it takes more than that. You've got to line up your need with your numbers. It's like going on-line in the cosmic Internet. You have to find your way through setup strings, com-port settings, baud rates, interrupt conflicts . . . quite a bunch of stuff. Interactively—"

"Forget about it," I said, and we trudged on uptown. Aaron would probably pass Headbloom's quiz on just what I'd told him about the book.

We were coming up on the Natural History Museum.

"I ought to drop in here for a data search," Aaron muttered. "Maybe a little Emotional Component."

"Aaron, not the Natural History Museum." We do about a half dozen school field trips to this museum every year, and I was up to here with it. And on a sunny Saturday?

"Why, Aaron?"

"I need all the information I can get for my computer-camp project," he said, not looking at me.

But the guard at the main entrance took one look at

Ophelia, and we weren't going in. You don't take a dog into the Natural History Museum. It's mostly bones in there anyway.

Dinosaur bones.

"This computer-camp project of yours," I said. "It's not about dinosaurs, by any chance? Tell me it isn't. We're sixth grade. We should be over dinosaurs by now. They're like Power Rangers."

Aaron strolled over to a bench outside the museum. He walks funny, like a duck. We sat down. Ophelia settled at our feet. She glanced at my ankle.

"Aaron, dinosaurs have been extinct for a million years. Let's just get on with our lives."

"Sixty-five million years, actually," he said, "and that's what my computer-camp project is about."

"We know they're extinct, Aaron. Have you seen one lately?"

"But why, Josh? That's the question of the ages." He tapped his forehead. "Why did this great doomsday of prehistory happen?"

I didn't know, but Aaron was going to tell me.

"Picture it." He threw one small leg over the other. "This giant asteroid, maybe five miles across, maybe ten, comes hurtling into the earth. And *pow*."

"Is this a theory or real?" I said. I try to be skeptical.

"Real," Aaron said. "They found the crater down in Mexico. It was over a hundred miles in diameter."

"Was the asteroid in it?"

"No, it vaporized. That's where the theories come in. One is that clouds of dust and sulfuric acid blew all around the world, shut off the light, lowered the temperature, and did in all the dinosaurs. The other theory is that the asteroid's impact set off volcanoes on the other side of the world. They poured so much junk into the air that it was good-bye, dinosaurs. Either way, a K-T boundary happened."

"K-T?"

"Cretaceous-Tertiary. A layer of clay covered the earth there—sort of asteroid droppings. And this layer was loaded with iridium."

"Which means?"

"Which probably means we're talking outer-space stuff. The rock that formed above the K-T boundary doesn't have a lot of fossils. Now we're talking Tertiary period."

"We're talking way over my head, Aaron. Where does your computer-camp project come in?"

His eyes shifted. "I'm working on a formula that's half-fiddled already. It's a sixty-four-character combination of numbers and letters, clustered, with—"

"But what's it for? Don't tell me it's supposed to reorganize your cells back in time sixty-five million years to check on the weather. I don't want to hear that."

"Okay." He shrugged and gazed off into space, maybe outer space. "Anyway, it's only a theory. I'm just doing a spreadsheet on it for the computer-camp people."

By the way, Aaron's voice is changing. It's changing, and he's shorter than I am. I don't think this is fair, but it's happening. Most of the time he talks in a regular sixth-grade alto. Then his voice hits a sound barrier and drops to baritone. He sounds like his dad, like a miniature Mr. Zimmer. Then sometimes in the same word he's both alto and baritone. It's like listening to the Vienna Boys' Choir.

"Come on. Let's go home. There's nothing to do in this town. We'll grab a giant hot dog from the guy with the cart."

"I'm a vegetarian," Aaron reminded me.

"You can have the sauerkraut."

We came back past the Dakota. I tried one more time to get Aaron's mind away from the K-T boundary and off dinosaurs and his formulas. I told him a story about the ancient apartment building, the Dakota. It was a story of the weird and unexplained.

"Hey, Aaron, one night late this guy who lives at the Dakota was coming home. He looked way up at the windows of his apartment, and he was amazed. There were people in his living room having a party or something. All the lights were on. And there was a big old-fashioned gaslight chandelier blazing away in the middle of his ceiling. Are you listening?"

"Yes."

"Well, he couldn't believe it. He thought he was looking at the wrong windows. He counted up. He counted over. They were his windows, and guess what."

"What?"

"He didn't have a chandelier. Never had. So he raced upstairs and opened the door of his apartment. It was dark. Nobody was there. No chandelier. Is that eerie or what?"

"Was he a substance abuser?"

"Aaron, you're no fun anymore."

"Just because I don't believe that lame story about a ghost chandelier?"

"It could be true. Strange stuff happens. There have been sightings."

"Nothing scientific," Aaron said.

"You want some frozen yogurt?" I said.

By the time we got back to our building, Ophelia was beginning to whine. I hadn't shared any of my hot dog with her, and she knew her walk was over. In the park she'd been prancing on ahead, showing off, looking down her muzzle at other dogs. Now she was pulling back. We got her past Vince and into the elevator.

Then it happened.

Somebody stepped into the elevator right on our heels. And not just anybody. It was Miss Mather. She's the one who lives under us and says we're jumping on her head. She's the meanest woman in Manhattan. Which is saying something. She doesn't like anybody, and she has a dog.

Sort of a dog. It's a shih tzu, so it looks like a small mop with paws. It doesn't bark. It screams. Miss Mather isn't that big either, and she's incredibly old. They built the building around her.

Suddenly the elevator was completely filled up with three people and two dogs. Ophelia whipped around, spotted the shih tzu, and lunged. When Ophelia attacks, she attacks. The pom-pom on her tail goes straight up. Her floppy ears seem to stand straight out, and she's all teeth.

The shih tzu's eyes bulged through all the hair on her face. She screamed, backpedaled, rear-ending the door which was closed now, and tried to climb Miss Mather's leg.

"Nanky-Poo!" Miss Mather screamed. Nanky-Poo was halfway to her knee, but Miss Mather was kicking Ophelia with her free foot. Where else but New York are you going to see an eighty-year-old woman kick-boxing a poodle?

I dreamed Saturday night. I was falling as usual. This time I was plunging out of the Fuji Film blimp and down to the K-T boundary. It looked like concrete. I was between a blimp and a hard place.

Sometimes I wake up before I land. This time I hit the ground. Except it wasn't the K-T boundary. It was a soccer field. I bounced at the foot of a terrible monster that ought to be extinct.

It was Miss Mather. Nanky-Poo was with her, and in the nightmare Nanky-Poo was as big as a horse. They both started kicking me.

3

How Fossils Are Made

On Sunday night I was looking ahead at another five days of school. At least I never have to decide what to wear. We have a dress code at Huckley School: black blazer, blue-and-white Huckley tie, big shirt, gray flannel pants, any shoes but sneakers. I had my dress code laid out on a chair, so all I have to do in the morning is walk into it.

I was in bed and thinking about turning out the lights when Heather barged into my room. She feels free to drop in anytime, but don't try going into her room. Heather goes to the Pence School for Girls, which has a dress code too: a lot of Pence plaid and only one earring per ear. But for the last month of school they can wear what they want to. It's a big privilege, and we'd been hearing about it all weekend.

Heather was wearing combat boots and a long, flimsy skirt with flowers on it and an oversized denim jacket that sort of filled out her chest—everything from Urban Outfitters.

"What do you think?" she said to the chair, where my school clothes were laid out. I'd arranged them so well, she thought they were me.

"I'm over here in bed, Heather."

"What do you think?" she said, whirling around.

"I think it's still night. It's not time to go to school yet."

She had on a lot more eyeliner than Pence or Mom allows. "Josh, I'm rehearsing. Like a dress rehearsal." She spun around twice and held up handfuls of her skirt. "Of course, I'll be wearing a backpack to complete the look."

"You look like a street person," I said.

"Like you know all about girls' clothes," she said. "It's what everybody will be wearing."

"So isn't that the same as a uniform?"

"Let me explain," Heather said. "When adults decide what you wear, it's a dress code, and it's wrong. When Muffie McInteer decides what you wear, it's fashion, and it's right."

Muffie McInteer is Heather's friend for life. Last winter her friend for life was Camilla Van Allen, but Heather switched. She made herself at home on the end of my bed. She hadn't come in here to discuss fashion. Her eyes were bright and beady. "I've got summer sewed up."

My eyes narrowed. "How?"

"Two words," Heather breathed. "Muffie McInteer." She let that soak in. "Her parents have a big house on Dune Road out in the Hamptons. Servants. Heated pool. And a beach full of boys. This is where I'll turn thirteen. I'll enter my teen years with a perfect tan line and a boy on every dune. Parties, Josh. Summer nights under the moon. Perfect?"

"Perfect," I muttered.

"What's Pencil-Neck doing this summer?" Heather asked. Pencil-Neck is her name for Aaron. Don't ask.

"He's probably going to computer camp," I mumbled.

Heather heaved up a big sigh. "So that leaves you, Josh."

"Don't start, Heather," I said. "We got through the weekend without hearing Mom's plans for me."

"What choice does she have?" Heather said. "It's too obvious to mention. You're going to soccer camp. You must look hilarious in soccer shorts. It's hard to know *what* to do with you. You're at the awkward age."

"Give me a break, Heather. I'm only fifteen months younger than you."

Heather sighed again. "It's different for a woman, Josh."

Then she left.

Aaron wasn't on the bus Monday morning. He goes in early to work on the terminals in the media center. If he's more than five minutes from the nearest computer, he starts keyboarding the air. Then he seemed to have signed himself out of his morning classes. At noon I checked the salad bar in the lunchroom, but he wasn't there. The trouble with a best friend is that when he's not around, you don't have anybody. Later on in life I think you can have more than one friend, but not in sixth grade.

As I reached for a tray, I got a sudden flash.

What if Aaron had gone into the media center this morning and started fiddling this new formula of his . . . and it had worked? What if he'd had a cellular meltdown or reorganization or whatever? What if he'd e-mailed himself back to the dinosaurs or someplace?

I panicked.

Frederick "Fishface" Pierrepont was behind me in line. I nearly trampled him as I headed for the door. I pounded down to the media center. The terminals are in a back room Aaron calls the Black Hole. There was a sign on the door:

BOTH COMPUTERS DOWN

But that didn't mean anything. Aaron puts up that sign whenever he doesn't want to be interrupted. Really scared now, I turned the knob.

Aaron was in there, and so was Mrs. Newbery, the media specialist. She was hunched over one of the keyboards, and Aaron was standing beside her. They were eye to eye, and he was giving her a lesson.

"It's a piece of cake, Mrs. Newbery," he was saying. "The instructions for loading the disk are inside the front cover holder. You've inserted the CD-ROM in the drive, right?"

"Did I?" Mrs. Newbery said faintly.

"Okay, now choose from your File menu and type 'd colon backslash setup' in the Command line box. No, wait. Don't press Enter till you've clicked OK."

"Okay," Mrs. Newbery murmured.

"So now the rest of the instructions are right there on the screen. All you have to do is double-click the icon, and you're in business."

Mrs. Newbery's hands hung in the air. Aaron patted her shoulder. "Let's go over it one more time. A bit is a piece of information, remember? And a byte is the basic collection of eight bits that makes computing possible. Are you with me on this?"

The back of Mrs. Newbery's head quivered. She turned around and saw me at the door. She seemed relieved. "That's about all I can absorb today, Aaron. You two better cut along and get some lunch."

We left.

"Adults," Aaron said out in the hall. "You just can't make it simple enough for them. Mrs. Newbery doesn't know a bit from a byte. She doesn't know a binary code from Bart Simpson. She doesn't—"

"Okay, okay," I said. "Aaron, you scared me bad. I thought you'd . . . like, vanished."

His pink eyes peered up. "Cut school?"

"Not exactly. I thought you'd been fooling with your computer-camp formula, and it might have . . . I don't know."

"Dialed me into the cosmic Internet and faxed me back to the Tertiary period?" Aaron blinked. "Josh, I'm only in sixth grade. That's post-graduate-level work. All I'm aiming at is a spreadsheet."

The lunchroom lines were short when we got there. I went for a taco, and Aaron made himself a salad that was mainly bean sprouts. No wonder he's beginning to look like a rabbit.

This being a boys' school, there was food on the ceiling, and you couldn't have heard your own Walkman. Let me explain about Huckley. You've got the lower school, which is up through fourth grade. You've got the middle school, which is fifth through eighth, and the eighth graders run it. After that it's the upper school unless you go away to boarding school. Except for Aaron, who'll probably go straight on to the Massachusetts Institute of Technology. Where they can study him. We settled at the end of a table.

"The trouble with you, Josh, is that you think computers can do anything." A bean sprout hung down from Aaron's mouth and moved when he talked. "You have a very simple view of the whole process."

"My trouble is," I said, "I'm looking at a solid summer of soccer."

I shouldn't have mentioned it.

A bunch of people loomed over us. A fist hit the table. Our trays jumped. We looked up, and it was Daryl Dimbleby—Terrible Daryl. We don't have a gang at Huckley. We call it student government. Daryl's the middle-school president. He won in a landslide because he shaves.

Nobody around here is named Daryl, but I think he's a foreign-exchange student from someplace like Oregon. He's built along lumberjack lines, and he's a very clean-cut, good-looking guy until you come to his eyes. Then you see he's mean as a snake.

He wasn't alone. He never is. He had his eighth-grade peer group with him and two or three of the larger seventh graders, and Buster Brewster. Buster is the biggest kid in sixth grade, and bad to the bone.

"Sixth graders, right?" Daryl snapped at us.

He knew.

"Why are you two still in the lunchroom?" he said. "Spell it out for me. If there's anything I hate to see, it's sixth graders lolling around in the lunchroom like they own the place." Daryl's snake eyes bored down into us. "What's our motto for sixth graders? Remind me."

"Eat it and beat it," Aaron mumbled.

"You got it," Daryl said. "So get out of here and stop cluttering up the landscape with your miserable small bodies."

He stroked his stubbly chin. "Wait till we get you two into soccer camp. We'll either make men or mincemeat out of you. Take this as my personal pledge."

"Actually," Aaron said in his changeable voice, "I'll probably be going to computer c . . ." But his words trailed away. His bean sprout hung limp.

Daryl planted a pair of massive fists on his hips, so his whole peer group did too. "What's the school rule? Let's hear it."

So his whole bunch chanted:

"Eighth grade leads,
Seventh grade follows,
Sixth grade crawls,
Fifth grade wallows."

Even Buster Brewster got the words right.

Aaron and I were more than ready to take our miserable small bodies out of there. But we probably weren't moving fast enough. Anything could have happened to us. Then Coach Trip Renwick entered the lunchroom.

This is his first year on the Huckley faculty. He still wears his Dartmouth sweatshirt. The whistle around his neck hangs from a lanyard he probably made as an Eagle Scout.

"Code alert," Daryl muttered. "It's Coach Renwick." His peer group unclenched their fists. Buster straightened his tie.

"Hey, fellows, how's it going?" Coach Renwick boomed, and they all beamed innocently at him. The sparkle off Daryl's white teeth was blinding.

Aaron and I escaped.

On the way to History it hit me like a ton of bricks. In regular P.E. class we play soccer by grade. The worst that can happen is that Buster Brewster will kill you. Buster likes to inflict as much pain as possible, even on his own team. But at soccer camp . . .

"Aaron, Terrible Daryl Dimbleby is going to soccer camp. Why didn't I think of this? We'll be living under his rule."

"What we?" Aaron said.

School went on forever that day. Then when Aaron and I got home, Miss Mather was in the lobby, talking to Vince. Nanky-Poo too. She was hanging from Miss Mather's shoulder in a carrier bag. Nanky-Poo's face was sticking up from the bag. When she saw Aaron and me, she remembered Ophelia and screamed.

"There they are now," Miss Mather said to Vince. She pointed an old finger at me. "That is the boy who jumps on my head." She pointed at Aaron. "That is the boy with the attack dog."

An attack poodle?

"Young man," she said to Aaron, "I have lived all my long life in this very building, and I have never known such an outrage. I have alerted my lawyers. That animal you harbor is a public nuisance. It is clearly out of control."

Which is true. Ophelia flunked out of obedience school.

"And it will simply have to be put to sleep."

I thought about Ophelia asleep on her silk cushion up in the penthouse with her muzzle between her paws. Then I realized that Miss Mather meant something else. Aaron and I edged around her to the elevator.

I was going to push twelve when he said, "You can come on up to the penthouse if you want to." This was more like the old Aaron, and I didn't have any plans. I'd finished *Time and Again* and was as ready for the quiz as I'd ever be.

As soon as we were in Aaron's room, he booted up his computers. Lights flashed. Menus came up. Various voices spoke. Monitors glowed. Aaron limbered up his hands by playing over the keyboards. Then he was pointing and clicking and doing all the stuff he does. He was calling up his computer-camp-project formula. It began to flash on both screens and the added-on videos. Letters of light, figures of fire, visuals—clustered. Even Aaron couldn't hold all this in his head. He peered. He squinted. He double-checked.

When he seemed satisfied, he turned around to say, "We never finished lunch, did we? I'll see what's out in the kitchen." Aaron's idea of junk food is tofu and carrot curls.

Then it came to me. It was a really bad idea, but it filled up my brain. Here right in front of me in an empty room was the formula that could send Aaron to computer camp.

What if his formula got changed a little bit? What if just one of his digits was off? What if he showed the computer-camp people a bunch of no-brainer nonsense for his project?

They wouldn't take him.

I'd have a friend to go to soccer camp with. We could get stomped together.

I know, I know. But I was desperate. Terrible Daryl Dimbleby had pushed me over the edge.

Then I noticed that my hands were reaching for the keyboard. They didn't know where to begin. Even computer-literate people wouldn't know their way around Aaron's totally personalized and encrypted blendo-technopolis. It was like his brain—totally unexplored.

I pointed and waited. I clicked. A finger of mine touched a key. One of the digits in Aaron's formula winked out. I clicked OK. I entered a different digit, I forget what, and pressed Enter.

I stepped back to watch screens all over the wall blink and make the change. Aaron came in the door behind me. I jumped a foot. He brought in two lo-cal power drinks and a plate of raw turnip sticks.

I looked at this snack. "Is that it?" I said. "What are we, gerbils?"

I watched him chew for a while. I didn't feel good about what I'd done to his formula. You don't have a lot of guilt in sixth grade, but you have some.

Aaron didn't look too innocent himself. He was up to something. He hadn't invited me up here to watch him eat turnip sticks. He chugalugged his power drink and stood up.

"I'll need you to stand right there in the middle of the room," he said, not looking at me.

"Wait a minute, Aaron."

"I'm going to try a dry run on this formula. Remember it's just theoretical. It's only happening on the screens."

"Then why do I have to be here?"

"You're just backup," he said. "In case something happens to me, which it won't."

"What am I supposed to do if it does?"

"Use your initiative."

But I remembered that thanks to me, nothing would happen, probably.

He was staring at one of the screens. I could tell from

the back of his head that all the compartments in his brain were fully engaged. Now he was working up his Emotional Component. All his thoughts were going in one direction, which mine never do. He was lining up his numbers with his need. He was being very creepy.

He pressed Enter. Deep in its heart, a microprocessor clicked. A robot voice said,

PROCEED RETROACTIVELY

With a few moves Aaron scrolled his formula to the tops of the screens and entered another set of digits. The whole wall seemed to think about this. The voice said,

QUADRATIC QUOTIENT SEARCH
NOW SCANNING EXPONENTIALLY

"What's that in English?" I asked.

"Mathematically, I'm halfway back to the K-T boundary," he said. "I told you it wasn't interactive. I told you I had the bugs out of my formula. With any luck, I'll be able to display a computerized schematic of the prehistoric world that'll knock the socks off of—"

I saw it on the screens first. But they were only reflecting the room. The walls wobbled. The floor warped. We staggered. Even Aaron's wall-sized technopolis was changing its shape, softening. Digits ran together.

Winking lights merged. Schematics got all tangled up with each other. The whole room was coming apart around us like wet Kleenex.

I'd made the formula misfire. Were Aaron and I going back to the Tertiary period? We were in the penthouse of a building that wouldn't be built for millions of years. We'd fall sixteen floors to dash out our brains on the K-T boundary.

I made a grab for him. "Aaron," I screamed, "I have a confession to make."

But who heard? The walls were like screenwire now, and the wind howled in. We were turning and turning through time and space.

I had one final thought. This is how fossils are made.

4

One of Those Days

I was flat on my back, and all the vertebrae in my spine seemed to be separate. I need to watch this. There's a history of back trouble in my family. My hands felt around. I was stretched out on sand.

I didn't want to move. I wanted to spend history here. Out of the corner of my eye I saw Aaron's miserable small body lying on the next sand dune. I saw his shape in the dark. I didn't see breathing.

Then he sat up and looked around. He saw me. "We've gone to the beach. Why?"

"Do I know?"

"Why are you even here?" he said. "I bet you were standing too close to me. I told you to stay in the middle of the floor."

"Aaron, the whole room fell apart. Maybe the whole world."

"Can you sit up?"

I could if I took it easy. Sand was drifting into my pants.

"Aaron, where are we?"

He was pulling on his chin. "Sand, sea, sky. It could be the Tertiary period. It could be later than that. Hey, it could be the future if my formula really went cuckoo."

It was a warm evening, too quiet except for the lapping of the waves. It wasn't a bad place to be, exactly, if we only knew where.

"I think we're being watched," Aaron said in a spooky whisper. "In fact, I'd put money on it."

"Knock it off," I said. "I'm already scared."

But I knew it was true. My flesh crawled. We made ourselves look around. From over a high dune two glittering black eyes in a ghostly white face were looking down at us. Nothing human. It would have scared the pants off R. L. Stine.

Aaron whimpered. Or maybe it was me.

The lips on the face curled back. Light shone on fangs. Then the thing bounded up and started skittering down the dune on all fours. Her rhinestone collar winked. She had her imported Italian-leather leash in her mouth.

Ophelia.

Aaron's head dropped into his hands. Ophelia bounded up to nip at his knees.

"I don't believe this." Aaron spoke through his fingers. "Get down, Ophelia. Heel."

But was she ever glad to be out. She was dancing

around, kicking sand in our faces, having a great time. Aaron reached in his pocket to see if he'd brought a Baggie. "How could my formula go this wrong?" he moaned. "How could it interactivate Ophelia?"

"Aaron, I have a confession to—"

"You know what happened, don't you?" he said.

"Yes, Aaron, I do. When you were out of the room, I—"

"We're here because of *Ophelia's* Emotional Component," he said. "Something went haywire in the microprocessor, and it lined up my numbers with *Ophelia's* need. All she ever wants to do is go out for a walk."

"Aaron, she wasn't even in the same room with us."

He nodded. "She's either on her cushion in the living room or at the front door with the leash in her mouth, waiting to go out. See how far wrong my formula has gone? Boy, do I have some numbers to recrunch. If my formula's picking up on Ophelia's need, it could pick up on anybody's."

"Aaron, you may have crunched your last number. You may have diddled your last data. We don't know where we are. We could be in some other time zone. We could be in some other time. We could end up with our faces on milk cartons. Aaron, we're *missing*."

He climbed to his feet like an old man, which he sort of is. "Come on, give me that leash, Ophelia," he said. She can nip you and keep the leash in her mouth at the same time. But he got it on her collar. It was a strange scene. Aaron in Huckley dress code with Ophelia on her leash, and we could be in Saudi Arabia or somewhere.

I got up and we started trudging. First one dune and then another. We came to some tall grass bending in the breeze. Aaron examined it, and Ophelia did her business. We moved on. Ophelia pranced ahead, showing off as usual.

Aaron's foot hit something in the sand. He reached down and dug around. Then he held it up: an empty Diet Pepsi can.

"Well, that narrows down the time frame," he said.

Pretty soon we came to a lifeguard's tower. Then we began to see roofs and finally a sandy sidewalk. We started walking along a street. There were some big shingled houses in long yards under trees. At one place they were having a party. Porsches were lined up outside. Then we came to a public phone under one of those round plastic domes.

"This must be an upscale community," Aaron said. "Nobody's stolen the phone book."

It was the Yellow Pages for Netherhampton, Long Island.

We were about a hundred miles from home.

"The Hamptons," we said. "We're in the Hamptons."

"But why?" Aaron asked. "Ophelia just wants to go to the park. She wouldn't know the Hamptons from a hole in the ground."

"Forget Ophelia," I said. "What time is it, anyway?" We checked our watches. It was a quarter to six.

"Anyway, we know where we are," he said. "We can take a train home." We pooled our money to make sure we had enough. "I've got a phone card. You can call home and say we'll be late. And then your mom can call my mom."

"Why me, Aaron? We're going to have to tell big fibs, because who'll believe the truth? Why don't you call your mom, and she can call my mom?"

"It's my phone card," he said. So I guess that meant I had to call my mom. It was eerie. Half an hour ago I thought we might be eaten by dinosaurs on a prehistoric beach. Now I was direct dialing via AT&T. Heather picked up on the first ring.

"Muffie?"

"Josh."

"Why aren't you home? It's almost dinnertime. Mom's beginning to get steamed." Heather sounded happy.

"I'm with Aaron. I guess we lost track of time. We're . . . still at school. We're . . . studying."

"Please," Heather said. "If I couldn't lie any better than that, I'd never get to go anywhere."

"No, really. But listen, Heather, was there a power outage in our building?"

"I thought Aaron was with you," she said. "No, the electricity's on. What's your angle here? Are you going to try to tell Mom you're late because of a black-out?"

Aaron nudged me. "And call Aaron's mom," I said. "Tell her we've got a lot more studying to do—at least

40

three hours—for a quiz tomorrow in Mr. Headbloom's class." I hung up fast.

"What quiz?" Aaron said.

We found the Long Island Rail Road station without too much trouble. We bought our tickets from a guy at the window and only had to wait a little while for the train.

"Heather says there wasn't a power outage at our building."

"So?" said Aaron.

"Aaron, you were there. The whole room blew apart. The walls fell off. Your technopolis experienced extreme meltdown."

He put up a small hand. "That was just our perception of what was happening. It was our cells reorganizing. It wasn't the room disintegrating. We were. My equipment will be fine, but I have a major fiddle to do on that formula. Back to the drawing board."

"About the formula, Aaron. I—"

But the train roared in, and we got on. Ophelia rode free.

At Remsenburg a few more people got on. A guy in a cap came around to punch our tickets. Ophelia lunged at him but missed.

We didn't get back to Manhattan till after ten. Then we had to get a cab from Penn Station because you can't take a dog on the subway, unless it's a guide dog, which, believe me, Ophelia isn't.

It had really been one of those days. I was wiped out. And I'd had to booktalk Mom all the way through Jack Finney's *Time and Again* to prove to her Aaron and I had been studying for the quiz. And still she wasn't satisfied.

"Josh, don't think you can stay out till all hours. Just don't start with that."

But Heather of all people came to my rescue here. "Mo-om," she said, "you don't need to know where we are every minute. Especially me. If you're going to be on our case all the time, we'll end up druggies. Especially Josh."

I couldn't wait to get into bed. Then I had to shake all that sand out of my pants. Then could I sleep? Forget about it. My cells just wouldn't settle down. Finally as I was drifting off, the truth hit me.

I sat straight up in bed like Aaron on his dune. Heather. I remembered what Heather had said. It was like she was right here in the room, repeating herself. "Two words," she'd said. "Muffie McInteer." Heather wanted to spend the summer at Muffie's house in the Hamptons. The one with the servants and the heated pool and the boys on the beach. Parties.

It was probably my fault, but Aaron's formula had picked up not only Ophelia's need, but Heather's too. It was a two-for-one deal. We got Ophelia's body and Heather's wish, which was better than the other way around. Though when you think about it, Ophelia and Heather aren't that different. They both whine. They both think they're great looking. And they both want to go out all the time.

The force field or whatever had reached four floors down to our apartment and Heather's room. Probably at the very minute Aaron was entering his formula, Heather was thinking about the Hamptons, counting the days.

In a way it was more interesting than Aaron's boring computerized schematics of dinosaur days.

But where would it end? I really wondered. Then I was sound asleep.

Aaron wasn't on the bus Tuesday morning, missed homeroom, and barely made it to Headbloom's class for the quiz. I know Aaron. He'd been hacking all night, and he'd come to school early to keep on working at the terminals in the Black Hole. He looked terrible. Red hair, greenish face, staring eyes, and stumbling around. He kept running into desks on the way to his.

Class was about to start, but I couldn't wait. As he lurched past me, I grabbed him by the dress code. "Aaron," I muttered. "One word. Heather. It's *Heather* who thinks if she doesn't spend summer in the Hamptons, then her life is over. Nobody needs like Heather. Your formula picked up on *her*."

"Oh, right," he said. "I figured it was something like that."

Which was the thanks I got.

"Meet me in the Black Hole at lunch," he said. "We're on a roll."

I decided not to.

Leave Aaron alone. Let him refiddle his formula back

to normal and send himself to computer camp. Who cares? Let him fax himself to the moon. He's more trouble than he's worth. He looks funny, and he acts funny. If he wasn't my best friend, I wouldn't have anything to do with him.

Then I realized I was going to have to eat lunch alone in the lunchroom while Terrible Daryl and his peer group made mincemeat out of me.

The BOTH COMPUTERS DOWN sign was on the door as usual.

I entered the Black Hole.

Mrs. Newbery wasn't around. Aaron was by himself between the terminals with formula on both screens. "Come in," he said, not looking around, "but don't think."

"What's that supposed to mean?" I said, with my back against the door.

"Just keep your mind blank," he said. "You know, pretend you're in Math class. I don't want us projecting any particular need close to these terminals. They're not state-of-the-art anyway. They're practically vacuum tube."

Now he was hunched between the screens, one hand on a keyboard, one hand on a mouse. A pointer drifted along and stopped.

"See that digital cluster? A bug, maybe even a virus, is skulking around in that particular part of the formula, but I can't—"

"Aaron, I—"

"But look what happens when I bypass." The screens blanked, and something else popped up.

"What is it?"

"Just what it looks like," he said. "A chemical equation."

We don't do chemistry till upper school.

"It either expresses the sedimentary composition of the K-T boundary or something else. I'm not sure. It could be the chemical contents of a dinosaur's stomach. Who knows? But anyway, I'm getting there. Computer camp, here I come."

He spun around in his chair. "If it's lunchtime, why aren't we eating?"

"We should have gotten there earlier," I reminded him. "You know how Daryl—"

Aaron stood up. "Josh, do you know how much tuition our parents pay to send us to this school? We're talking five figures here. We're laying out that kind of money, and we can't have lunch? Please."

This was tall talk from the shortest kid in class.

"Are we going to let Daryl—"

"And his peer group including Buster," I said.

"And his peer group including whoever deprive us of basic nutrition and a balanced diet?"

It was a good speech. I wished it was coming out of somebody bigger. I wished it hadn't been half alto. But Aaron was right, and I was hungry.

We started to leave for the lunchroom while we still had the nerve. But Aaron went back to store his formula.

Then it happened.

And this time it hurt.

The walls bulged. The floor buckled. The terminals blurred. I seemed to be seeing Aaron through one of those fun-house mirrors. He'd laid one finger on his keyboard, and it was all happening again:

Cellular reorganization

Personal disintegration

Interactivity

I went blind for a minute. Pains shot around me where I'd never had them before. Feet, spine, you name it. Somebody had thrown a rope around my neck and was trying to strangle me. Somebody—Daryl?—had me in a hammerlock and was pinning my shoulders. But at least I wasn't falling this time. In fact, I seemed to be getting higher in the room.

Then it all stopped.

There was a little steel-gray haze drifting in the room. At least it was still the Black Hole and not the Hamptons. But why was I hurting so bad?

And where was Aaron?

5

A Couple of Complete Strangers

Not that I was alone. I was hurting too bad to think, but somebody was in the Black Hole with me. At first I thought I knew him. Then I didn't. Over by the computers was this big, red-headed guy. Upper school at least. He shaved. In fact, he needed a shave.

There was something else you really noticed about him. He was wearing Huckley dress code like anybody else. But it was six sizes too small for him. His shoulders were busting out of his blazer. His big wrists hung way down from his sleeves. His pants stopped a foot from the floor. He swallowed, and the collar button on his shirt cut loose and flew over his Huckley tie.

I was still being strangled, but it wasn't Daryl. It was my shirt. My collar button popped too. We both watched the buttons roll around the floor.

"Who—" we both said, except it wasn't my voice.

"Aaron?" I said in my dad's voice.

He blinked, and they were still Aaron's eyes, pink and dazed.

We were both twice our size and trapped in our dress code. I could get my tie loose, but my pants were cutting me in half. Aaron winced and stooped down to untie his shoes. His pants made a ripping sound. He eased out of his shoes, and feet popped out. They couldn't be Aaron's feet. They were about size eleven. There's always a hole in his sock. A huge toe with a thorny nail poked through.

I couldn't bend over without snapping every stitch of my clothes, but I could kick out of my shoes. Then my feet sort of sprang to life, and they were as big as Aaron's, maybe bigger.

"Look at you," we said.

"Who are we?" we said.

"What have we done?" Aaron smacked his forehead.

I didn't know. I couldn't think. I scratched my chin. I needed a shave. And another thing, we were tall. Aaron was five ten, easy, and I was looking down at him. I was so tall that when I looked down, I got dizzy.

Aaron's stubbly face fell into his big hands. "No," he said, "no, no, no, no."

"What happened, Aaron? You know. You have a theory." I couldn't get used to my voice. It was like my dad was sitting on my tongue, talking out of my mouth.

"Emotional Component," he said, "too close to the keyboard."

"But my mind was a blank," I said.

"Not when we were going to lunch," he said. "Then we were really worried about Daryl's peer group, right? What did we both want at that moment?"

"I don't know," I said. "Didn't we just want them off our case?"

"Go with that thought."

"Oh. We both wished we were bigger than they are. And older. We wanted to be—"

"That's it," Aaron said. "We had the same thought at the same time. We wanted to be upper-school size. We wanted to be seniors."

The sacred word *seniors* hung in the air. My dress code was binding me bad.

The bell rang, and lunch was over.

"Aaron, how are we going to explain this? I wouldn't know you if I met you on the street. We're a couple of complete strangers. How can we go to History like this? How can we go home? This isn't the Hamptons. We can't just take a train."

"No," he said, "but it's the same principle, except instead of Ophelia and Heather, it's us. Our need combined spontaneously with my formula. That virus in it made it so interactive, it's almost infectious. I'm thinking radioactivity. I'm thinking—"

"Aaron, shut up."

He thought for a minute. A big new vein in his forehead pulsed. Then, making senior gestures with his ham-sized hand, he said, "Here's the plan: Forget about History class. We couldn't pass ourselves off as us.

49

Anyway, look how we're dressed. We're ridiculous. We wait till the bell rings again. Then we give it another ten minutes. Then we make a break for the upper-school locker room. After they've changed for P.E., we'll get into their lockers and take some clothes that fit us."

"Is this stealing?"

"It's borrowing, and do you have a better idea?"

We waited. Another bell rang, and the school settled down for afternoon classes. We waited some more, and I couldn't get used to this body. It bulged all over, and my head was so far from the floor, I nearly had a nosebleed. Then at the last minute we remembered our sixth-grade shoes and hid them in a file drawer. As Aaron said, if Mrs. Newbery found our shoes but not us, it would just deepen the mystery.

"Let's synchronize watches," he said at the door. Luckily both watchbands were expandable. We had wrists like tree trunks. "We do this at a dead run," Aaron whispered. "If Mrs. Newbery's at her desk, sprint right past her. She won't know us anyway."

When Aaron opened the Black Hole door, we ran into each other. Then we started galloping through the media center. Mrs. Newbery wasn't around, which was just as well. I was pretty sure that somebody was in the book stacks, but I didn't really look because everything was a blur. We weren't used to being this big. It was like running on stilts. All four of our legs got tangled up, and we came crashing down in front of the Leisure Reading revolving rack. We were both grunting. Also, our dress code strangled us all over. When we got up, I heard the seat of Aaron's pants go completely.

The upper-school locker room is in the basement at the other end of school. It was two flights down, and we fell twice each. Our sock feet were like flippers. Then we were thundering down an endless corridor, taking huge strides, following the smell of the upper-school locker room. Then we were in it, and it was empty. The big guys were all over at the soccer field in the park.

"Aaron, we don't know the combinations of any of these locks."

"If they're anything like the middle school, half of them are broken." He ran a gigantic hand along the locker doors. He jerked one open, then another.

And inside . . . big dress code.

"Aaron, what if they don't fit?"

"Josh, this isn't The Gap. We're not shopping."

The upper-school guys' books were in their lockers with their names on them. "Hey, look," I said. "This is Harrison 'Hulk' Hotchkiss's stuff."

"And I'm getting Otis 'Stink' Stuyvesant's stuff," Aaron said. "We're in luck. These are two of the bigger guys in upper school."

I pulled out a huge blazer. "Whoa," I said.

"Don't dawdle," Aaron said. "Get naked and get dressed."

I hadn't thought about getting naked. I don't usually think too far ahead.

I wrestled out of my little blazer. Taking off my shirt was like shedding a skin. When I peeled off my pants, my door keys popped out of a pocket and fell on the floor. I swept them up. Hanging on a hook in the locker were Hulk Hotchkiss's big underpants. I wasn't too crazy about wearing somebody else's used underpants. But my sixth-grade pair really had me tied in knots.

Aaron was down to his underpants too. We turned our backs on each other. Finally we were free.

Then we said, "Wow."

6

Better Than Grown

We could keep our own socks. They stretch. Hulk Hotchkiss's shoes were a tight fit. I could have used a size larger. The hardest part was knotting our Huckley ties with our big hands. We had fingers like sausages. Aaron was really slow. Until just lately, his mom's been tying his tie for him. When we were finished, we looked each other over. It was fantastic. It was unbelievable.

My fully formed heart pounded in my well-developed chest. "Okay," I said, "where do we go from here?"

"We get out of the locker room before anybody comes back," Aaron said. "We get out of school."

"Just walk out?"

"Senior privileges," Aaron said.

Huckley School is a block away from Central Park. Halfway to the corner, we met the upper-school guys coming back.

Stink Stuyvesant and Hulk Hotchkiss led. Everybody was in Huckley sweatshirts and shorts, swaggering toward us. I started to get in the gutter like you have to do when you've got upper-school people coming at you.

"Forget that," Aaron said, and we held our ground. They walked around us, the whole class. They didn't know us. They couldn't place us. But we were the same size as they were, bigger than most. It felt great.

Hulk Hotchkiss had brushed right by me. Little did he know he'd just walked past his own underwear.

We crossed Fifth Avenue, and then we were in the park. Aaron seemed to have something in mind. Like a plan. Now we were coming up on the soccer field. We sat down on a nearby rock and pulled up our huge knees.

Suddenly it was great. It wasn't even weird anymore. It was the perfect spring day, and we weren't in class, and we were practically grown. Better than grown. We were in upper school.

"How old do you think we are, Aaron?"

"I put us at seventeen, pushing eighteen. I'd say we were looking at colleges about now."

We sat there and felt the sun on our big stubbly faces. We basked. "Aaron, we're adolescents, and we didn't have to get here. We didn't have to do the whole puberty thing. We didn't have to do the pimple thing. We didn't have to—"

"Hold it a minute," he muttered.

People were beginning to trickle onto the soccer field from Fifth Avenue. Small, spindly people in droopy shorts were dragging net goals.

"Is that our Gym class?"

Aaron shook his head. "Our class is last period. This is the eighth grade." It was. Trip Renwick in his Dartmouth sweatshirt was in the lead. Next to him like an assistant coach was Daryl Dimbleby.

We watched while Daryl assembled two eleven-man teams and ordered the real runts to the sidelines. We noticed how he put all his peer group on his own team, making sure the other team could be systematically stomped. We watched Daryl rule while Coach Renwick stood around, taking roll or whatever.

We watched the game kick off.

Then Aaron climbed off the rock. He slipped out of the blazer and rolled up Stink's sleeves.

So I did too. "What are we doing?"

"We're going to level the playing field."

"We're what?"

"We're going to show Daryl how soccer's played."

"But Aaron, we don't know. We're terrible at soccer."

"We were," he said.

He flexed his thick neck and then his big elbows. He hugged one knee and then the other in a warm-up.

So I did too. Then we started walking toward the game.

We weren't suited up, but our ties said we were from

Huckley. And who's going to keep a couple of upper-schoolers out of an eighth-grade game? Please.

Most of the guys who weren't on Daryl's team were already flat on the field, clutching parts of their bodies. We came in on their side.

The next minutes went really fast. I was feeling my way, trying to throw my weight around. Aaron got into it. Where his coordination came from I can't tell you. But he had control of the ball and was ankling it down the field, making magical moves with his vast feet through a forest of knobby knees. His fiery hair flashed in the sun, and now the ball was bouncing off his big shoulders, off his heels, you name it. Aaron was steamrolling the peer group. Daryl was screaming for time-out.

Then somehow I myself was pounding up behind Daryl, and Aaron was bearing down on his front like an express bus. It was amazing how small Daryl actually was. Shrunken, nearly. My Mighty Morphin kick went wild, and Hulk's thick shoe connected with the back of Daryl's shorts. It really lifted him. Aaron seemed to confuse Daryl's head with the soccer ball itself. The sound of their colliding skulls echoed.

Daryl went down hard, and a circle of his sidekicks formed around him. We'd given Daryl a taste of his own soccer. Coach Renwick's whistle cut through the chaos.

Aaron and I made a run for the rock. And we could run like deer. We grabbed up our blazers and kept on going. We didn't stop till we were in sight of the Metropolitan Museum of Art.

Then we were leaning against a couple of trees, getting our breath back. The adrenaline was thundering through me.

"That was great," I gasped. "You want to go back for last period and get Buster?"

"We made our point," Aaron said. "We got better things to do with our time."

"How much time do you think we have?"

It was almost the old Aaron again, because his sausage fingers were beginning to keyboard the air. Old habits die hard.

"Cyberspatially, we could stay like this. I'm talking numbers, not need. But the Emotional Component wears off." Aaron tapped his forehead. "After all, the human brain is the ultimate computer."

"Are you a hundred percent sure that we're . . ."

"Bidirectional? Yes."

"So what are we talking here—hours, days?"

"It varies," Aaron said, meaning he didn't know. "Wanting to go back could speed up the process. Like if we both concentrated, we might—"

"Frankly, my heart wouldn't be in it, Aaron. I'm not ready to give up all this." I pointed at my body.

"That's because you never think ahead," he said. "Next class period we're still absent. After that we're at large. We're fugitives. Also, we could go back to being eleven within the next couple of minutes. Think about that."

I stared. "You mean we'd be back to our miserable small bodies, but wearing these big clothes in the middle of Central Park?"

"Exactly. Our best bet is to get home and hide in our rooms till it happens. Anyway, this condition is caused by a virus loose in my hard-drive memory. The sooner I get back to my technopolis, the better."

Mention of the virus I'd caused shut me up till we got to the little pond where kids sail their boats. Aaron was keyboarding the afternoon air. We were taking long strides in our big shoes.

"I can't see it," I said. "Today we're getting what we wanted. When we went to the Hamptons, we got what Ophelia and Heather wanted."

"My formula's cuckoo," Aaron said.

"I know that. But Ophelia came with us to the Hamptons. Why didn't Heather, not that I wanted her?"

"We went because we were standing too close to my equipment. And Ophelia wasn't that far away. Ophelia's mind is probably better focused than Heather's. Who knows what kinetic powers dogs have? They've got a lot of untapped potential. Dogs can hear sounds that humans can't, right?"

"Do I know?" I said. "Am I a poodle?"

"Careful," Aaron warned. "Just don't say things like that around my PC."

I hadn't thought how we'd get past Vince the doorman until we were already in the lobby. But Miss Mather was there, bending Vince's ear. Nanky-Poo was hanging in Miss Mather's carrier bag, but neither one of them screamed at us as we walked past.

In the elevator Aaron said, "Your mom won't be home from work yet, will she? I'll stop by your place in case. If she's there, we'll have to duck out and make a run for the penthouse. We can hide in my room."

"But for how long, Aaron? My mom's going to want me home for dinner, believe it. She can't see me like this. She won't know me. She'll think some senior got in her apartment and ate her little boy. What's she going to say, 'My, how you've grown since breakfast'? Please."

Aaron shrugged. Then we were at my front door, and I was slipping a quiet key into the lock.

The apartment seemed empty at first. But in the front hall we heard a voice from the living room. And a squeal.

"This is the truth, Heather, and I'm never wrong. Every boy in America is going to be at the Hamptons this summer. I'm talking upper school. I'm talking boarding school. Heather, I'm talking *college*."

Heather squealed. I know her squeal.

"Summer boys in Speedos, Heather. Trust me, we're going to have a beach full of Brad Pitts."

Heather squealed.

I whipped around and ran into Aaron. "It's Heather and Muffie McInteer. They're out of school early or something. They're in the living room. We can't get past them."

"Forget about it," Aaron said and gave me a shove. I staggered into the living room doorway, in plain view of Muffie and Heather.

If you know Heather, you'd recognize Muffie. Heather copies everything from her: clothes, hair, boots, you name it. Heather's a Muffie clone. They were on the sofa with their combat boots tucked up under them. They looked at me and blinked.

Before I could think, Aaron stepped up beside me. We filled the doorway.

Heather's and Muffie's jaws sagged. "Who—" said Heather.

"Wow," said Muffie.

I don't think too well on my feet. But Aaron adjusted Stink's tie and made his move.

"Hel-lo, ladies," he said in a rich baritone. "Allow me to introduce myself." He put out a square hand.

Muffie and Heather were all eyes.

"I'm Stink Stuyvesant," Aaron rumbled. "Call me Stink. I'd like you to meet my friend, Hulk. Hulk Hotchkiss."

We didn't look anything like Stink and Hulk. But we were their size, and Muffie and Heather wouldn't know them from Adam anyway.

Heather's hand came to rest in Aaron's large mitt. Muffie's came out for mine. We bowed slightly.

Muffie's never at a complete loss for words. She scanned our ties. "It's Stink Stuyvesant and Hulk Hotchkiss. Everybody knows them, Heather. They're Huckley upper school." Heather didn't have a hope of recognizing me. She couldn't tear her eyes off Aaron.

"What hunks," Muffie murmured.

7
What Hunks?

Muffie couldn't drag her eyes off me, and Heather wouldn't let go of Aaron's hand. They'd spent all afternoon discussing older guys, and suddenly two appear before them. Magic.

"What . . ." Heather said, stunned. "How . . ."

"We found your front door unlocked," Aaron lied in a deep voice. "You need to watch that. There are a lot of crazy people out there these days."

Heather gaped. Personal safety was the last thing on her mind.

"We dropped by on the off chance we might find Josh and Aaron around," Aaron said to her.

"Who are Josh and Aaron?" Muffie asked. Boys buzzed in her brain.

"Josh is my geeky little brother," Heather explained. "Aaron is his nerdy friend, Pencil-Neck."

"Is Josh the kid with the dweebish voice who keeps answering the phone when I'm trying to call you?" Muffie asked.

"Ummm," Heather replied, lost in Aaron's eyes. "Why do you want them?"

"It's like this, Heather—it is Heather, isn't it?" Aaron's hand slipped smoothly out of her clutch. "Hulk and I are cocaptains of the Huckley upper-school soccer team. I don't know if you know that. We've had a certain amount of publicity." Aaron stubbed his toe modestly in the carpet. "And we're scouting the most promising young players in middle school."

"Then why do you want to see Josh and Pencil-Neck?" Heather was confused.

Aaron looked at me. "The sister is always the last to know, right, Hulk?"

I nodded. Muffie's eyes were burning asteroid craters in me.

"You see," Aaron said, chopping the air with a big hand, "Aaron and Josh have a lot of raw talent, on and off the soccer field. We think they both have leadership potential. We see great things for them when they get to upper school: soccer team, student government, you name it."

Muffie and Heather swayed.

"But, hey, Hulk." Aaron gave me a power punch on the arm like a mature Hardy Boy. "We better get going. Every minute counts. Right?"

He turned back to Heather. "Tell your brother we dropped by, Heather. It is Heather, isn't it?" Then he added, "And tell Aaron if you run into him."

Another couple of squeezes on their hands and we were out of there. But we weren't through the front door before we heard serious squealing from the living room.

Out in the hall take-charge Aaron said, "Ring for the elevator and press Penthouse."

On the way up I said, "Aaron, you were awesome. You're going to be really good with girls."

He grinned, which he never does in real life.

"I mean it," I said. "Sometimes the nerdiest guys in middle school turn out to be . . ."

But his grin was beginning to fade.

Getting into the penthouse was a piece of cake. The housekeeper was in the kitchen. Aaron's room seemed like a closet now that we were in these big new bodies. He clumped over to boot up his workstation. He entered his virused formula, and it came up on the screen.

"It's time to go back to the way we were," he said. "We really want this, am I right? Our parents better not see us like this. We both want this real bad. We agree, okay?"

I nodded.

"So stand with me between the keyboards. I'm sensing radioactivity here. I'm sensing a matrix. Let's line up our numbers with our need."

I stood there. "I wish I may," I muttered, "I wish I might—"

"Josh, this isn't like wishing on a star. Really concentrate."

We did our best, but nothing happened. Aaron ran a finger around Stink's collar. "I could fiddle the formula while we're both standing here, but I better not. We could be one digit from dinosaurs. Maybe we're rushing things."

I wanted to hide till it happened. I wanted to phone Mom and tell her I was sleeping over at Aaron's, but I had the wrong voice.

Finally I went home, right past his housekeeper, who doesn't notice too much, and down the back stairs to our kitchen door. Aaron wasn't that sorry to see me go. He couldn't wait to do a major revamp on his formula and micromanage his technopolis. I saw him eyeing the soldering iron.

I made it to my room, and I wasn't in there five minutes before it happened. The whole room wobbled with my pain. Shrinking hurts just as bad as growing, maybe more. My ears rang. My cells raged. Then I was standing low in the room in these gigantic clothes. They were like a clown suit. Hulk's big blazer and the tip of his Huckley tie swept the floor with my little feet in his size twelves poking out beneath. I could have turned around in his shirt. I was ridiculous.

Then I fought my way out of this giant dress code. The underpants fell off me. I could walk out of the shoes. I grabbed a Bulls sweatshirt Dad had sent me from Chicago and a pair of my old jeans and my own sneakers and jumped into them. I hustled all Hulk's clothes into the closet. I was breathing hard.

My door opened, and Heather looked in. She was still starry-eyed from Stink Stuyvesant. "Yes, Mom, Josh is home," she screamed over her shoulder. "He's lurking in his room.

"What are you doing in here anyway?" she said to me.

"Homework," I squeaked in a dweebish voice.

"Please," Heather said, and left.

Right away my phone rang. I get almost no privacy. I answered and so did Heather from her room. You tell me how she got there that quick. We have separate phone lines and different numbers, but she gives mine out. And when she hears mine ring, she can switch over and horn in.

"Muffie?"

"Josh?"

"It's for me, Heather. It's Aaron. Get off the line."

We waited till she did.

"You back to normal?" he asked in a cautious, changeable voice.

"Yes," I piped. "About five minutes ago. It was like *pow*."

"Me too."

"Was it something you did?"

"Maybe. I was at my keyboards. I was interfacing. Maybe yes, maybe no."

"Anyway, we're back. We're bidirectional."

"I told you we were," Aaron said, "and when I get this fine-tuned, we're going to be able to—"

"Aaron, it's almost dinnertime."

"It is? Okay, but listen. Put Hulk's dress code in a shopping bag to smuggle into the locker room tomorrow. Somehow."

"Right," I said. "Over and out."

Mom doesn't do serious cooking on a weeknight. She's still winding down from a day at Barnes Ogleby. We had Stouffer's lasagne and a green salad. I missed being Hulk Hotchkiss. The fork felt big in my hand. But I was mainly relieved to be back to me. In sixth grade the less explaining you have to do, the better. Heather was at the table, toying with her lasagne, but she was mentally missing.

Mom likes a little dinner-table conversation if she can get it. "How was your day, Josh?"

My chin was down near the plate. "Pretty routine, Mom. It had its ups. It had its downs."

"Didn't you have a quiz in Mr. Headbloom's class? How do you think you did?"

"I probably aced it," I said.

Suddenly boys blurted out of Heather's brain.

"A couple of guys dropped by this afternoon," she mentioned casually. "Upper-school guys."

Mom sighed. "Heather, you know the rules. You're not to invite boys over when I'm not here."

"Mo-om, I didn't invite them," Heather said. "Anyway, they were looking for Josh and Pencil-Neck," which she hadn't meant to say.

"Really?" I said, looking up. "Who were they?"

"Two guys named Stink and Hulk," she muttered, "from Huckley upper school."

I let the fork fall out of my hand. "Stuyvesant and Hotchkiss?" I smacked my forehead. "They're only the two coolest guys at Huckley. What did they want to see me about?"

Now Heather had to say. "Something about soccer," she said, barely aloud.

I was halfway out of my chair. "They're scouting me for the upper-school varsity soccer team already?" I fell back in the chair. "I hadn't dared to hope."

Heather was totally disgusted now, and Mom said, "I didn't know you were that interested in soccer, Josh. I didn't know you were promising."

"Oh well," I said humbly, "I enjoy it mainly for the exercise."

Mom was really looking at me. There was practically a big question-mark floating over her head. "And Aaron's a good player too?" she said, mystified.

"He's not bad, Mom. He's shown a lot of improvement just lately."

By now Heather was close to tears. The conversation and Stink Stuyvesant were drifting away from her. Her geeky little brother was turning into a soccer star.

I have to say I was enjoying this. Then I realized what I was doing. I froze.

I was practically inviting Mom to send me to soccer camp all summer. I was practically signing my own prison papers. I shut up, but probably not in time.

8

How Bad Can It Be?

Something about the next morning didn't feel right. Something was missing, but I couldn't put my finger on it.

It wasn't Aaron. When I dragged a shopping bag full of Hulk's dress code downstairs, Aaron was on the curb with a shopping bag full of Stink's stuff. "Getting all this back will be the only tricky part," he said, "probably." Then the bus pulled up.

At school, half the eighth grade was on the front steps, making a circle around Daryl. He had a bandage on his head. "I was concussed," he told them. "It wasn't soccer. It was a mugging."

We went on inside. The halls were jammed. "Upperschool locker room," Aaron said, "and step on it."

We crept into the locker room like a couple of small

bag ladies. Nobody was around. We made our drop and left. On the way to homeroom I said, "How do we get our own clothes back?"

"We probably don't," Aaron said. "We'll have to tell our moms we outgrew them."

Then in homeroom an announcement blared on the P.A.:

JOSH LEWIS AND AARON ZIMMER:
REPORT TO THE HEADMASTER AT ONCE.

"Whoa," everybody said, and looked at us. Buster Brewster ran a finger across his throat. Buster has to report to the counselor every day because he's behaviorally disabled. But even he's never been to the headmaster. Some people don't even think he exists.

We went.

As we walked the last mile, Aaron said, "It can't be about Daryl's mugging. They definitely can't finger us for that. A couple of complete strangers did that."

The secretary in the headmaster's outer office looked over her glasses and nodded us to his door.

We went in.

It was a big, square room with class pictures on all the walls. The whole place smelled of fear. There were two items on a big polished desk. Behind it was the headmaster. He's an oldish guy, maybe eight, maybe ten feet tall, sitting back in his big leather chair. A shaft of morning sunlight glinted off his bald dome.

"Come forth."

We went forth with hung heads.

"Examine the evidence on the desk."

We looked, and there they were.

Our wallets.

That's what I'd missed this morning. When we'd put our clothes in Stink's and Hulk's lockers, we'd left our wallets in our pockets. With I.D. Home addresses. Next of kin. In Aaron's case, his A2Z e-mail handle. Full disclosure.

Aaron smacked his forehead.

"Explanation for this prank?"

Prank? I guess you could call it a prank. In fact, you might as well.

But we didn't have an explanation. Aaron was out of answers and as quiet as a tomb. I thought about pleading insanity.

"Claim your property," the headmaster said after a year.

We pocketed our wallets.

"About-face."

For one precious moment we smelled freedom. But two people were standing there when we turned around. I looked up six feet of backup dress code, and there stood Hulk Hotchkiss. Aaron looked up Stink Stuyvesant. If you ever wanted to make anybody feel small, this was the way. I hung my head. There on the floor in front of Stink and Hulk were our yesterday's dress code in little clumps. Everything but shoes.

"Apologies," the headmaster prompted behind us.

"Sorry, Hulk," I piped.

"Sorry, Stink," Aaron said, half alto, half baritone.

You couldn't blame Hulk and Stink if they were steamed at us. After all, they'd probably had to go home yesterday in shorts. But they're deeply committed preppies, and both of them are headed for Yale. They just put out big square hands for us to shake. Besides, what could they do to us without endangering their college admissions? Hulk's grip nearly broke every bone in my hand, though.

"Now pick up your own clothes and go," the headmaster said behind us. "Stink—I mean Stuyvesant's and Hotchkiss's dress codes have recently reappeared in the upper-school locker room. Otherwise we'd have to handle this as a theft instead of a . . . puerile prank."

Again we smelled freedom, until we got to the door. "And report back to this office immediately after school."

Homeroom was practically over anyway. We decided to take our yesterday's dress code straight down to the Black Hole and stash it with our shoes.

"What's puerile mean?" I asked.

"In our case, it means they got us on a misdemeanor, not a felony. How bad can it be? A few days of detention? They don't expel tuition payers. Maybe we can serve our time in the Black Hole. Maybe they'll release us in Mrs. Newbery's custody."

Aaron was still looking on the bright side. But knowing that we had to report back to the headmaster's office really made the day drag.

Rumors about us swirled through school. But the only thing everybody knew for sure was that we'd seen the headmaster and survived. We got some respect for this. Daryl let us eat lunch for the entire period. Buster Brewster wanted to be our friend—the worst kid in our grade wanted to bond with us.

Then we hit History. We made sure to get there on time. I made sure I went in behind Aaron. Mr. Thaw was taking roll already. He starts early. He looked up and said, "Zimmer. Freeze."

Mr. L. T. Thaw is Huckley's hardest teacher and the oldest. He should have retired long ago and gone to the Old Teachers' Home. But he thinks he owns the school.

Aaron stopped dead, and I walked up his heels.

"Number one," Mr. Thaw said, "you were absent without leave yesterday. You too, Lewis," he added, seeing through Aaron to me. "Number two, Zimmer, you were missing on the very day you were to give your oral report—a strange coincidence."

Come to think of it, this was true. Everybody in class had been assigned a U.S. president. We'd been giving oral reports on them all year long. I'd already done Chester A. Arthur. Now we were up to Franklin Delano Roosevelt.

But Aaron had forgotten. We'd both had a lot on our minds.

Mr. Thaw's old eyes pierced him from under craggy brows. "So I suggest that you make up for lost time, Zimmer, by giving your report now."

There Aaron stood, defenseless, not a note in his hand, not a printout on his person.

"Whoa," the whole class said.

"Now?" Aaron said in a small voice.

Mr. Thaw nodded. He meant to hang Aaron out to dry, and the whole class settled down to watch. I slipped into a seat. Aaron shrugged and strolled to the front. People in the back of the room stood up to see. Every eye was on him. He looked back.

"Picture it," he said, borrowing a gesture or two from Stink Stuyvesant. "The American nation on its knees from the Market Crash of twenty-nine and the Great Depression. Breadlines and banks closing, Hooverville shantytowns blossoming in every vacant lot. Onto the scene for the election of 1932 comes Franklin Delano Roosevelt, son of an aristocratic Hudson River Valley family and distant cousin of Theodore."

Here Aaron nodded down a row to Fishface Pierrepont, who had already given his report on Teddy Roosevelt.

"F.D.R.," Aaron said, plucking facts out of the classroom air, "unhappily married member of the Harvard class of ought four, served as New York state senator and assistant secretary of the Navy, and was governor of the state during the first of his four successful runs for the presidency. Moving right along, we come now to the New Deal, the Tennessee Valley Authority, and—"

"Very well, Zimmer," Mr. Thaw said in a weary voice. "Resume your seat." He squinted down the rows. "Who's doing Truman?"

I was impressed and annoyed. When Aaron resumed his seat, I gave him a poke. "How do you *do* that? How can you call up all that data?"

"It's common knowledge," he muttered back.

Aaron got us through History, and we hadn't been missed in Math yesterday. Coach Renwick hadn't minded us cutting soccer. Then we came to the end of the day, and it was time to report back to you-know-who.

"Look, how bad can it be?" Aaron was still saying as we slumped down to the headmaster's outer office.

The secretary was at her desk. Two other ladies were sitting along the wall. My head was hanging, but I looked up.

"Mom," I said.

"Mom," Aaron said.

Our moms were there, and they had the look of parents who'd already seen the headmaster.

"Josh," Mom said, "I've had to take time off from work."

"Aaron," Mrs. Zimmer said, "this was my court time at the tennis club."

We both smacked our foreheads. We were being released in the custody of our moms.

And another thing. We got our quizzes back on *Time and Again* from Headbloom that day. I got a B. Aaron got a B plus.

9

The Threshold of a New Frontier

Older guys beginning to hang around Heather and the house?

Me turning into a troubled kid pulling pranks at school?

Dad still out in Chicago?

With all this, Mom had a lot on her mind. She and Dad speed dialed all weekend. Then on Sunday night he gave me a jingle. Usually I wait for his call. That night I wasn't so eager.

"Josh, what's this prank you pulled at school all about?"

"Dad, I'm thinking puberty."

He sighed all the way from Chicago. "You know what I'm thinking? I'm thinking you're acting out because I'm not there."

"That's a good thought, Dad. Come on home."

But he said he couldn't do that. He was working around the clock on the Lucky Mutt account.

The whole situation was left up to Mom. She said I was grounded until I could come up with a complete explanation for swapping senior dress code for my own—full disclosure.

If you ask me, a sixth grader is grounded most of the time anyway. In my case it meant cutting down to an hour of TV every night, so I was in my room a lot. I may be the only kid at Huckley without TV in his room.

I didn't see that much of Aaron, but we probably needed to take a breather from each other. At school he was in the Black Hole. Then he'd tear home to his technopolis. He basically grounded himself, but he'd call me up from his room in the evening.

"Picture it. When I foolproof this formula, look what we've got."

"What? Free trips to the Hamptons and the headmaster's office?"

"Think bigger, Josh. We're standing on the threshold of a new frontier, and I'll be a shoo-in for a Westinghouse science scholarship. Most of the great discoveries in science are accidental. What I've stumbled onto here is essentially a new formula. Once I've got it vaccinated for viruses, we can dial ourselves into the cosmic Internet and go with our every need. Past, future, even lateral moves. This could rank right up there with the discovery of radium and call waiting. Josh, what we may have here is the Great Interactive Dream Machine."

Aaron was so pleased with himself and his new discovery, it was too late to confess I'd helped. "What about your old formula? The one that does schematics of dinosaurs to send you to computer camp?"

"I've got that on the back burner." Aaron sounded vague. "I'll get back to that."

I let him rave on about his dream machine. What choice did I have?

I was leading a pretty quiet life, but Heather dropped in one night. Being grounded didn't mean I could keep her out of my room. I was in bed reading when she barged in and flopped down. Her eyes were bright and beady, but worried.

"Two words," she said. "Hulk Hotchkiss."

The R. L. Stine jumped in my hand. I marked my place in it.

Heather moped. "Muffie's beginning to get letters from him."

"She lies," I said without even thinking about it.

"Muffie would never lie to me," Heather said. "Do you think she's lying?"

I nodded.

"How would *you* know? She says Hulk's letters are pure poetry." Heather gave herself a hug. "He can't wait for summer either. It'll be the two of them under the stars on the same dune. Her mother will hate it. Perfect?"

"Too good to be true," I said.

Heather sighed. "So I was wondering . . . do you ever see anything of Stink Stuyvesant?"

I shrugged. "I haven't seen a lot of him lately."

Heather swung her combat boots off my bedspread and started for the door. "Well, the next time you run into Stink," she said somewhat hopelessly, "tell him . . . like hi." She hung on the doorknob. Then she left.

I read until my light began to flicker and dim and go on and off. So Aaron was still awake, up in the penthouse tinkering his technopolis. I closed my book and decided to call it a day. R. L. Stine has given me some of my all-time most exciting and interesting dreams.

The big bombshell of the week didn't go off till after dinner the next night.

I was in the living room, selecting from *TV Guide* for my sixty minutes of viewing. Mom was there on the sofa, making a stab at conversation.

"So what's been happening, Josh?"

"Mom, not a lot can happen to you when you're grounded," I said. "I think that's the point."

The doorbell rang, and Heather rocketed from her room to answer it. Mom and I waited.

Heather came back, something stunned in her eyes. Filling the doorway behind her was a guy about six four. Well-gelled blond hair slicked back. Good tan for this time of year. Shoulders out to here. He was wearing three shades of Banana Republic beige over a muscle shirt.

I heard Mom swallow.

He loomed into the room and stuck out a hand like a shovel. "Mrs. Lewis? Trip Renwick here."

It was Coach Renwick. I knew that. But he wasn't wearing his whistle and Dartmouth sweatshirt. And what was he doing here, anyway?

Coach Renwick is a good-looking guy, but I never noticed how good-looking till I saw him impacting Heather and Mom. Heather was still weaving in the doorway. Trip had to remove his hand from Mom's clutch. "Hey, er—Josh, how you doing?" he said, scanning over my head.

To fill up his soccer camp, he was making calls on parents. He was conducting a house-to-house search. And he was really scraping the bottom of the barrel if he wanted me. Also, what woman could say no to him?

Mom was beginning to recover. "I understand that Josh is turning into a very talented player," she said.

Coach Renwick looked puzzled. "Josh? I mean sure, he's beginning to show . . . some stuff. A full summer of soccer, and he'll—"

"I'm afraid Josh can't go to soccer camp," Mom said.

I blinked.

"Ma'am?" said the coach.

Mom reached over and patted my hand. "I'm sorry, Josh. I know what this means to you."

She turned to Trip, who was mentally checking me off his roster. "As you may have heard," Mom said, "Josh has had a minor discipline problem at school. His dad and I mean to nip this in the bud. Josh is going to have to earn my trust back. I mean to keep an eye on him this summer."

Heather snickered.

Trip was trying to think. "Well, ma'am, we take discipline cases at soccer camp. Buster B—"

"You won't be taking Josh," Mom said. "He'll be staying in the city. He'll be going to summer school."

Heather snickered.

"So you see, Coach Renwick," Mom said, "Josh's summer is sewed up."

Trip Renwick was getting up to go. Relief was flooding through me. Give me summer school any day. You come home at night.

Heather showed Trip the door and came back. "Send *me* to soccer camp," she said. "What a stud." Then the phone rang, and that would be Muffie, so Mom and I were alone. The *TV Guide* was still in my hand.

"Not too disappointed about soccer camp?"

"Mom, I'll take my medicine."

"We've got another problem," she said. "Major. Heather's going to Pence summer school."

"Whoa, Mom. She's planning to spend all summer in the Hamptons with Muffie McInteer. I vote we let her."

"Heather's not ready for the Hamptons," Mom said, "and she needs summer school. Her grades are terrible."

"I can believe it, Mom. Heather thinks the Gettysburg Address is where Lincoln lived. She thinks grammar is your mother. But I don't want to be around when you tell her."

"Neither do I," Mom said, "but it's got to be done."

"Tonight?"

Mom nodded and ran a weary hand around the back of her neck. "I've put it off as long as I can."

"I think I'll turn in early," I said.

In my room I gave Aaron a jingle. "Seen anything of Trip Renwick?" I said when he picked up.

"He was around earlier," Aaron said, "but I answered the door and headed him off. The guy must be desperate. What's that screaming in the background?"

"Heather. Mom's just told her she isn't going to the Hamptons. She's going to Pence summer school. I'm going to Huckley summer school, so I don't have to go to soccer camp."

"How'd you work that?"

"By rifling Hulk's locker and getting caught, basically."

"Cool," Aaron said. "Speaking of summer, I'm not going to computer camp."

More relief flooded through me. "How come?"

"I missed the deadline for applying. We've been so busy lately, it got right by me."

This happens to Aaron. He's so busy thinking, he doesn't think. This happens a lot.

"Forget about it," I said. "Go next year. Do summer school with me."

"Might as well," Aaron said. "So what else?"

"Muffie says she's getting letters from Hulk."

"But in her head you *are* Hulk."

"Believe me, I'm not writing them. Muffie's either

writing them to herself or telling big fibs to Heather."

"Women," Aaron said.

When Heather finally stopped screaming, I crept out of my room. She was barricaded behind her door. Mom was in the living room, just sitting. She's pretty even when she's tired, and she looked pretty tired.

Then it hit me. I come up with a good idea once in a while.

I strolled into the living room. "Bad scene with Heather, Mom?"

"The worst yet."

"Mom, I'll cut you a deal."

She sighed. "At least I have one child willing to negotiate."

"What if I can get Heather to stay home and go to summer school and even be happy about it?"

"Dream on," Mom said.

"Mom, I can do it. But here's the deal. I'm not grounded anymore, and I don't have to explain about Hulk's dress code because I'll never be able to come up with a good explanation for that. Deal?"

"Deal," Mom said. "Let's hug on it. But I'll believe it when I see it."

I went to my room. I had a letter to write.

I did a rough draft. The next day I showed it to Aaron. He did some editing and ran a spell check on it. Then he printed it out on a sheet of Huckley School stationery we found in Mrs. Newbery's desk before homeroom. I told Aaron he'd have to work up a signature and sign it.

Dear Heather,

You probably get a lot of letters from guys, but I hope you won't mind one more. I ran into your brother, Josh, at school today. I enjoy talking soccer with him. He happened to mention you'd be in town this summer.

I'm a little tired of the same old faces at the Hamptons myself. Like enough already, you know what I mean? Maybe we'll run into each other.

Heather, do you believe in fate?

Sincerely and I mean it,

Stink Stuyvesant

We mailed it at lunch.

10

The Watcher

The rest of the school year was pretty routine. As soon as Heather got her letter from Stink Stuyvesant, she was a new woman. There was hope in her heart, and she even started making her bed. I didn't know how long this could last, but Mom was impressed.

"Josh," she said, "I hope I never need to know how you did that."

"I hope you don't either, Mom," I said. "Really."

On the last day we have the All-School Field Day in the park. There's the traditional faculty-against-upper-school annual softball game, which Aaron and I snuck out of after the first inning. We went over and sat on our rock and really kicked back.

This was going to be our first real summer in the city. Up till this year, we'd gone away to kid camp. Aaron

and I had gone to Camp Big Wampum in the Adiron-
dacks, where it took him years to pass the swim
test. Heather had gone to Camp One-a-Bee in the
Ramapos.

But all that was behind us. It wasn't the same as being
seniors, but it was getting there. I thought summer
looked like smooth sailing.

I should have known better.

That very night I got a jingle from Aaron.

"Come on up," he said.

His telephone voice sounded worried. "My parents
have gone to bed, so come up the back way. I've
left the kitchen door unlocked. We may have a
problem."

"What we?" I said.

But I figured I'd better go.

Even the back stairs seemed more deserted than
usual. It was summer in the city, and a lot of people
were away. Our building felt big and old around me,
like the Dakota. I kept looking over my shoulder. Then
I was creeping past Ophelia's dark sleeping shape on
the way to Aaron's room.

His head was outlined against the screens. The bluish
light turned his red hair purple, and the back of his
neck glowed. He never tanned, not even at Camp Big
Wampum.

"Take a squint at this," he said, never moving. He
clicked Read Old Mail on his menu bar. E-mail came
up:

Hey, A2Z man,

Fast-forward gamma-force greetings!

Been anybody lately? Next time you seniorize, factor in compatible dress code. You modem morons looked ridiculous.

Better yet, try foolproofing your stone-age formula before you polymorph your miserable small bodies again.

See you in cyberspace, suckers,

Happy hacking,

THE WATCHER

I couldn't believe my eyes. I couldn't swallow. The hair on my arms would be standing up if I had hair on my arms. I clutched my forehead. Something evil was on the screen.

"Aaron," I whispered, "somebody's onto us."

He sat there slumped in his swivel chair. "I feel violated," he said.

"How could anybody—"

"A thousand ways," he said. "I could be accessed by any on-line maniac."

"But they're not just accessing your PC. They're accessing *us*. That crack about miserable small bodies sounds like Daryl."

"It could be anybody in the lunchroom that day," he said. "When Daryl talks, people listen."

"So that narrows it down to—"

"A lot of people," Aaron said.

"But who could know about that day when we seniorized? Nobody was around."

"The Watcher was," Aaron said in his creepiest voice.

11

Now or Never

We only had a weekend between the end of school and the start of summer school. I don't remember much about the days, but the nights were killers.

You know that kind of dream when you're in bed so you don't know you're dreaming? I mean you're not falling or anything, so you think you haven't gone to sleep yet, but you have? I had that dream for two nights straight.

I'm in bed, covers pulled up, looking down past my feet. There's Aaron—purple hair and the back of his neck glowing against bluish screens. He's busy interfacing with his technopolis. So how did he happen to move all his equipment and his swivel chair down to my bedroom? In dreams you don't ask. And it's very real—you know what I mean.

He's keyboarding like crazy, and it's just like the day-time Aaron. And I'm there in bed, right? Then out of the corner of my eye I see we're not alone. I'm sensing that over in the darkest corner of my room, the closet door is beginning to open. We've all had that dream, but I haven't had it since third grade.

So I think I better mention this to Aaron. That we've got company—that somebody's violating our privacy—that somebody's onto us. I want to be casual. I don't want to make a big deal out of this, so I open my mouth, but nothing comes out. I'm screaming down my throat, but there's no sound. Needless to say, I can't move.

All this time the closet door keeps opening. This dream is so real, I can hear the bottom of the door brushing across the rug. I can hear a hinge. Now my whole throat is a Carlsbad Cavern, and I'm screaming down it silently.

Also, I know that if I turn my head to see who's easing the closet door open, something really horrible will happen. I'll turn to stone or something. So I figure if I don't turn my head—or breathe—we're still okay. But I know the closet door is yawning wide. And with this third eye I seem to have in my ear, I see this shape standing there, filling up the whole closet door. I see this figure with my dress code hanging up behind him. I actually hear hangers jingle.

I know who it is, of course. I can just about hear his voice, a real metallic voice, saying, *Fast-forward gamma-force greetings,* because it's The Watcher. It's

The Watcher, and he's hacked into my bedroom, and he's the worst thing in the world. He's Mister Death.

And now my neck's in a vise, and some superior force is cranking my head around so I have to look at him and see who he is, though I know that if I can identify him, I'm doomed. Doomed, do you hear?

But I look anyway. It's that kind of dream.

At first I think it's Mr. Thaw from History class. He's that skinny and corpselike. But it's not him. Then I think it's the headmaster. He's that tall, but I don't know if he's bald because he's wearing a big hat, black as a bat, along with a big black shroud. So it's not the headmaster either. And then I don't want to do this, but I'm looking into his face for a positive I.D.

And he doesn't have a face. It's just smooth, shiny skin, glowing bluish from Aaron's screens. But he can see us, and he can seal our fate, and there's no escape.

Then finally I can scream, but Aaron still doesn't hear because it's morning, and I'm awake, sitting straight up. My bed looks like a battlefield, and I'm sweating buckets, and it's daylight. The closet door is closed, but still I'm not sure.

Two nights of this.

The third was the night before summer school started. I was doing sit-ups on my bedroom floor, fully dressed, putting off getting into bed and trying to wear myself out completely so I wouldn't dream anything. Mom's light was already out, and Heather was in her room in full eyeliner, waiting for Stink to call.

I couldn't take the pressure anymore. I punched Aaron's number. He answered the first ring, and I told him I was coming up. I'd had it with everything, and it was time to tell him we had to go completely out of business, computerwise.

In ten minutes I was up in his room. I didn't tell him about the dream because it wouldn't cut any ice with him, but I was really trying to talk sense to him.

"Aaron, we were getting into enough trouble even before The Watcher—"

"Watcher, smatcher," he said, cool as a cucumber. "There are a lot of electronic outlaws and owlhoots out there in cyberspace these days. We're talking wire fraud. We're talking an expanding menu of electronic snooping." He squared his bony shoulders. "I'm already working on a more sophisticated encryption program. Nothing is future-proof, but—"

"Aaron, the cat's already out of the bag. The Watcher—"

He waved a small hand. "Try to keep calm." His mind had already switched to one of its other compartments. "Let me give you a little update on my recent progress on the formula."

"Aaron—"

"It's nothing personal. I'm just downloading some imagery. I'm probably not pulling in enough power to interactivate a tenth of our body weight. Believe it."

I didn't even understand it. But now Aaron was back in business, playing his keyboards like a pipe organ and doing all the stuff he does. I edged back on his bed. The whole room hummed. His screens displayed something in a flash too fast to see. A curl of smoke rose from his set-top box. It was Frankenstein stuff.

But we were still there and in our regular bodies, so it was okay, right?

Then we heard a small scream.

Aaron's sneakers shot up. His arms flew out, and he was looking in his lap.

"Aaron. What?"

A weird and unexplained moment passed. Then he began to swivel slowly around in his chair. At first I didn't see anything but his face. He had that half-electrocuted look.

Then I saw something in his lap, something strange. A mound of matted fur. Two shiny marbles for eyes. A small bow on her topknot. A mop with paws. She looked around and screamed again.

Aaron's face fell into his hands. "No," he said, "no, no, no."

"Aaron, is that Nanky-Poo?"

"How many shih tzus do you know?" he moaned.

"Maybe she got in by herself."

"Are you kidding me? Like she pole-vaulted up and unlocked Miss Mather's front door? Then she got on the elevator and pressed Penthouse? And how do you think she got past Ophelia? Ophelia would have had her for dinner. To Ophelia, she'd be a Tender Vittle. Then what? She turned herself into a letter and slid herself under my door?"

We looked. Aaron's door was closed. Nobody our

age leaves his bedroom door open. "And how did she get on my lap? She didn't jump up. She materialized. Her need lined up with my numbers. It's Ophelia and Heather all over again. All Nanky-Poo wants is to go out."

Her pink tongue poked through her mustache. Panting lightly, she sank a small claw into Aaron's knee.

"It's my formula. I'm not getting anywhere with it. The Watcher is right. It's stone age. I'll have every dog in the building up here. They all want out. I'll have to open a kennel."

"Aaron, we've got to take her back. You know Miss Mather. She's probably dialed 911 already. She'll have us in juvenile court for dognapping. She'll have us in *family court*. Nanky-Poo is family to her. She'll alert her lawyers, and I just stopped being grounded."

Aaron and Nanky-Poo sat there. "We'd get caught," he said. "The woman sees through doors. It'd be a prank, our second offense. Why don't we just wait? This is only a minor glitch, probably—an electronic hiccup. As soon as Nanky-Poo's Emotional Component runs out, she'll probably cellular-reorganize back home on her own. She probably doesn't have much of an attention span anyway."

"Aaron, by then Miss Mather will have a dragnet thrown around the city. She'll be slapping up roadblocks at the bridges and tunnels with her bare hands. She'll be going door-to-door. Nanky-Poo is her whole life. They even look alike."

Aaron thought about it. He wasn't that happy about sitting around all night with a lap full of shih tzu. He handed Nanky-Poo to me. She peered at both of us. We were vaguely familiar, but she couldn't quite place us. Aaron dug around in his clutter and came up with a shopping bag from The Sharper Image. "Put her in this. She's used to a carrier bag."

We crept out through the dark penthouse and past dozing Ophelia. Then we were ringing for the elevator.

"Here's the plan," I said. "We push eleven. When we get there, you keep the elevator door open. I run out, drop the dog, ring Miss Mather's bell, and beat it back to the elevator, and you push Penthouse."

Aaron nodded.

Then the elevator door opened. And somebody was inside.

We blinked.

It was a little guy, not that much older than we are, not that much bigger. He was in some kind of costume: a short jacket with rows of brass buttons. On his head was a little round hat held on by a strap under his chin. He blinked back at us. He wore a glove on one hand.

We were in the elevator before we could think. But here's the really weird part. It wasn't our elevator. It was like a big birdcage. You could see out to the walls of the elevator shaft. There was a bench you could sit on.

Now the little guy in the costume was pushing a gate across the door with his gloved hand. "What floor, sports?"

We stood there stunned. Finally Aaron said, "Eleven," in a crackling voice.

We began creaking down. It was a ghost elevator

from the days before automation. The guy was a—what do you call it? An elevator operator. We dropped to eleven, real slow, kind of clanky.

"Have a nice night," Aaron said in a wobbly voice as we walked out past him in a dream. The door clanged shut behind us.

"Aaron. What?" Nanky-Poo was still swinging from my hand in her Sharper Image bag. She whimpered.

"This is going to be a tad trickier than we thought," Aaron muttered. We were standing in front of Miss Mather's door. But making a dog drop, ringing her bell, and making a break for the elevator wasn't an option anymore. We were on different turf now.

Aaron turned the knob, and the door opened. "Her door's unlocked?" I said. "She'd never leave it unlocked."

"They wouldn't bother to lock their doors in the olden days," he said. "Back then, the doorman and the elevator operator were protection enough. Besides, there'd still be cops on the beat."

"Aaron, what are you saying? Are you saying that—"

"We're going inside," he said. "We don't know who's in there. We don't know when it is. We don't know anything. We don't speak."

We teetered on the threshold. There was a front hall, dark, and past it the living room, lighted. We crept in. Nanky-Poo whimpered again and scrabbled around in the bag. We stood at the edge of the living room. Aaron stuck his head around the doorway. He went on. I followed.

We'd never been in Miss Mather's living room before, believe me. It was fairly nice: a big crowd of antique-type furniture and pictures in silver frames. Eerie, but what we were doing was practically breaking and entering.

I wasn't thinking a nanosecond ahead, but Aaron just stood there, scoping out the room. He pointed to one corner. There was a big vintage combination radio and stone-age record player. On the front it said Strom-berg Carlson. The radio dial was glowing, and from inside, a tinny voice was singing,

"There'll be bluebirds over
The white cliffs of Dover . . ."

There was a table by the sofa with a picture of an old man in a frame and a couple of magazines. Aaron's finger fell on *The Ladies' Home Journal* and moved to the date on it: February 1942. The cover on the *Life* magazine was about the fall of Singapore.

Nanky-Poo whimpered again. She didn't want to be here. Neither did I.

Aaron peered up at me. Then we heard the front door open. We jumped a foot, and the next thing I knew, we were huddled behind the sofa with Nanky-Poo in her shopping bag between us.

There was murmuring in the front hall. Then somebody said, "Hush. Papa will hear."

"Only a moment, dearest," a deep voice said. For a second I thought I knew that voice. But how could I?

If they come in the living room, we're dead ducks,

I thought. Nanky-Poo was *this close* to one of her screams.

Their voices came nearer. But then she said, "No, Teddy, you'd better go. It's hopeless. Truly it is. I'll write as soon as you are overseas. Tell me where to write, and I will. I'll—knit you a sweater."

"Margaret, for once in your life," he said, "you must think of what you want."

They seemed to be as near as the doorway.

"Darling, marry me now," he said, "tonight."

"Oh, Teddy, you know I can't. Papa—"

"Let me talk to him, Margaret. Go and wake him."

"No, Teddy," she said, panicky. "You know how Papa is. There would be a dreadful scene. I can't send you away like that. After the war when you come back—"

Aaron's eyes came up over the back of the sofa. So did mine. It was like we had to see them. They were standing in the doorway. She was a young girl, not very tall. Pretty. Her hair flowed down over her shoulders, and there was a flower in it. The skirt of her 1942 dress was short.

He held her in his arms. He was a lanky young guy in a World War II army uniform.

"Don't tell me you'll wait for me," he said in a harder voice. "It will be no different later, and you know it. Marry me now, Margaret. Fling caution to the winds. It is now or never."

She pulled back from him, and her face dropped into her hands. She had bright-red fingernails.

"Oh no," she said through her hands. "This is not how I will want to remember this moment."

As soon as she said that, it happened. Maybe her words made it happen.

It was like a 747 roaring through the room—that quick and that loud. It wasn't my cells reorganizing this time. It didn't hurt. It wasn't happening to me, but everything around us changed. The lights blinked and surged. The upholstery on the sofa back changed color. So did the walls. They'd been blue or something. Now they were white. The pictures on the walls rearranged themselves in quick moves. The magazines melted. The picture in the silver frame clicked. The old man in it became somebody else, a young guy. For a second I thought I recognized him, but how could I? We felt the sudden rush of air-conditioned air.

I looked over at the Stromberg Carlson, and now it was a TV—not new, but from modern times.

The room sizzled and settled. Our knees were on a different rug. Miss Mather was standing in the doorway, alone. All these years later, she was a little shorter. She was wearing a bathrobe and a nightcap with wisps of gray hair sticking out. When she began to lift her old face from her wrinkled hands, we ducked down.

But Nanky-Poo jumped out of her shopping bag. She waddled away, twitching her little flag of a tail, happy to be home now. She circled the sofa, heading for Miss Mather.

We didn't breathe.

"Naughty Nanky-Poo," Miss Mather said in her old voice. "I turn my back for . . . a moment, and you vanish."

We were looking under the sofa at them with our chins on the rug. Nanky-Poo's flag tail was all over the place. Her claws dug into the carpet. When Miss Mather's hand reached down for her, she ducked. Nanky-Poo was looking back past her tail, across the floor, under the sofa, at us. She let out her version of a growl.

Now she whipped around, and her weird little chin was on the floor, like ours. Her mustache drooped on the carpet, and her hindquarters were sticking up. Her tail was going like a windshield wiper. Her marble eyes were beady, zoning right in on us, letting Miss Mather know we were there. She was like a bird dog, and we were dead ducks.

Then we saw Miss Mather's robe being grabbed up. She made a dash for the fireplace. We heard her grabbing a poker out of her fire tools.

So this is how it ends, I thought. I'm fifty miles from soccer camp, and still I'm going to get my brains battered out.

"Door," Aaron said. Without a thought in our heads, we came out of a crouch, vaulted over the sofa, and made a run for the front hall. Aaron took a flying leap over Nanky-Poo, who was screaming in circles. I had the Sharper Image shopping bag in my hand. I guess I didn't want to leave any evidence.

"Halt!" Miss Mather yelled behind us. "This is a citizen's arrest!"

We hit the front door. There were three locks on it: high up, middle, and down by the floor. Light flooded the front hall, and we were trapped. I saw the shadow of a poker sweeping across the locked door.

12

Trouble in the Making

"Turn around nice and easy," Miss Mather said, "hands high, feet wide." We obeyed. The Sharper Image bag hung from one of my high hands.

The poker rested on Miss Mather's shoulder, and she gripped the handle with both hands. It was like she was coming up to bat. Her old eyes burned big holes in us. "You are the boy who—"

"Yes," I admitted.

"And you are the boy with—"

"Here," Aaron said, like she was calling roll.

"Back into the living room." Her poker pointed the way. We filed past her. Nanky-Poo sat in the doorway with crossed paws like she didn't have anything to do with it.

We settled on the edge of the sofa, and Miss Mather

THE GREAT INTERACTIVE DREAM MACHINE

bent over us, leaning on her poker. "How interested I will be in your explanation for this unwarranted intrusion. I will be glad to hear, and there is nothing wrong with my hearing. It is alibi time. What do you have to say for yourselves?"

My mind was a blank, like in Math class. Aaron cleared his throat and said, "We were returning Nanky-Poo. She got out, and we brought her back."

That was brilliant. It was even true. I held up the shopping bag to help explain.

"And how could Nanky-Poo get out of this apartment when the pair of you could not?"

The questions were getting harder.

Aaron shrugged.

"Are you suggesting that I let Nanky-Poo out myself?" Miss Mather's eyebrows climbed high on her forehead, making more wrinkles.

"Maybe Nanky-Poo got out when you went . . . back in your mind," Aaron said, stroking his chin.

Miss Mather's old eyes narrowed. "What business is it of yours where my mind goes, you cheeky boy? I am old. My mind often drifts back to . . . earlier times."

"But tonight you really went back," Aaron said, "big-time."

Her poker scraped. "What do you two know of going back? What are you, nine?"

"Eleven," we said, somewhat hurt. "Almost twelve."

Miss Mather didn't get it. She didn't know that Aaron's formula had reorganized her cells. She didn't realize she'd been cybernetically interactivated. How could she? She just thought she'd been remembering. Now she looked away.

"Perhaps I am older than I thought," she said to the room. "Perhaps the past has become too real to me. I might be slipping." She looked back at us. "Old age creeps up on stealthy feet. Then one day you reach for the past as for something you have . . . misplaced."

That was truly spooky and a little bit sad, but I wasn't so worried about the poker now. Miss Mather pulled herself together.

"I would never be so forgetful as to let Nanky-Poo out. I am not that far gone. You two got in here somehow by jimmying the locks on my door. There is no other explanation."

We jimmied all three locks? Inside locks with bolts?

"I have observed you both since you were infants. I knew even then that you were trouble in the making."

She touched her chin with one finger. Her nails hadn't been red for as long as we'd lived. "It is no use my informing your parents. They clearly have no control over you. I expect they are asleep in their beds this minute."

I hoped so.

"The trouble with children today is that they still have too much energy by bedtime. In my day, children were *tired* at night."

We sat there while Miss Mather decided what to do with us. I still thought she might call 911. I thought we might be booked on a breaking and entering. My hands tingled as they thought about being fingerprinted.

"You cannot walk out of here scot-free, of course," she said. "There is no question of that. I must think of a punishment to fit your crime."

She snapped her fingers. "Of course," she said. "I will put you in charge of taking Nanky-Poo on her afternoon walk, since you are both so interested in her welfare. She likes to get out, you know."

We knew.

"She must ride in her carrier bag, naturally. She isn't allowed on the sidewalk. The sidewalks are filthy now. But you may take her to a pleasant, grassy spot in the park where . . ."

"She can do her business," Aaron said.

"As you say," Miss Mather said. "Four o'clock sharp for the foreseeable future."

The foreseeable future stretched ahead of us for as far as we could see.

"Otherwise I shall have to call your parents in for a rather painful interview." Miss Mather turned on her heel back to the fireplace and replaced the poker with a clang. "And now you'd both better be off. It is well past your bedtimes, if you had bedtimes."

Then we were out in the hall, and my head was pounding. "Miss Mather every day at four o'clock? I'd rather be grounded. At least I was in Mom's custody. Even soccer camp doesn't look that bad to me now."

Aaron was doing his duck walk down the hall.

"And now what?" I said. "Is that little guy in the buttons and the hat going to be running the elevator?"

"Are you kidding?" Aaron said. "He'd be like seventy years old now and retired from some other job. He's probably down in Florida eating early-bird dinners. Josh, the last time we stepped on that elevator, it was 1942."

"So it's like that story I told you about the Dakota apartment building, when the guy looks up at his window and sees the chandelier from gaslight days. It's like that."

"It's nothing like that." Aaron rang for the elevator. "That was fiction. This is fact. That was rumor. This is real. That was myth. This is—"

"Aaron, talk to me. Tell me why. Ten minutes ago it was 1942. Now it's not. Spell it out."

"Electronically—"

"No. In English."

"Josh, the past, the present, and the future are a multiple program running concurrently, with peripherals. Lacking an electronic nudge, the human brain processes sequentially, a nanosecond at a time with tunnel vision. But all times are happening at the same time."

"Thanks a lot for clearing that up, Aaron."

The door opened, and it was our regular elevator, empty and automated. We got in.

"And tonight was the best example of electronically nudged, emotionally driven time slip we've had so far. Do you realize—"

"Aaron, all I realize is that so far we've been dropped on a dune; we've been nailed for pilfering upper-school lockers; and the meanest woman in Manhattan has just given us a life sentence with a shih tzu.

"Not only that, Aaron, but a really scary Watcher is monitoring our every move. Possibly as we speak."

That got to him. He glanced around the elevator like it might need debugging. His eyes were haunted.

"Aaron, let me give you some advice. Pull the plug permanently on your technopolis. Ban yourself from the Black Hole. Take up something else. Get a hobby. Get a life."

"You crazy?" he said. "Things are just getting interesting."

I got off at twelve. The next day summer school started. It's just one thing after another.

13

Backward Is Forward

In summer school you get a few people whose lips still move when they read. But a lot of us were just dodging soccer camp. We weren't a big group. Some of the other guys from our grade were Dud Dupont, Pug Ulrich, Wimp Astor, Zach Zeckendorf, and Fishface Pierrepont. It was a fairly laid-back atmosphere. The dress code was Huckley golf shirt and khakis. Without Daryl and Buster, a lot of the pressure was off.

You only do a couple of classes, so it's not a full day. I was in Mr. Thornburg's Math refresher class called "Discovering Decimals." Aaron did an independent study in the Black Hole on "Next-Generation Cybernetics." You can't do an independent study until upper school, but Aaron cut a deal. He has a lot of creative ways of keeping school from interrupting his studies.

For the other class though, everybody including Aaron had to do a History seminar with Mr. L. T. Thaw.

Mr. Thaw clutched his craggy old brow when he saw Aaron strolling in with his new IBM ThinkPad for classroom use. The ThinkPad replaced his old one-chip Toshiba laptop. Aaron has never been that popular with teachers for some reason.

Even before he could find a seat, Mr. Thaw was on his case.

"Our subject this summer is the 1940's and World War II, and so we will maintain military discipline in this classroom," Mr. Thaw announced in his croaky voice. "There will be no absence without leave. There will be no oral reports without notes. Deserters will be shot. This goes for everybody and double for you, Zimmer."

Aaron crumpled into the nearest seat, and Mr. Thaw cranked himself up at the front of the room: "December seventh, 1941, Day of Infamy, when the attack upon Pearl Harbor found America asleep at the switch . . ." Already he was beginning to drone.

He didn't run down till one o'clock. By then I could have personally consumed Cleveland. The school lunchroom wasn't open in the summer, but I was ready to hit the deli on Madison Avenue.

"You hungry?" Aaron said on the way out of class.

"I could eat."

"Because I want to drop by the Black Hole first."

He would.

Officially, the media center was closed, but they leave it unlocked for summer school. The headmaster's secretary is supposed to be the paraprofessional in charge, but she's never in there. To be on the safe side, Aaron had borrowed Mrs. Newbery's keys and had a set made for himself.

He hung the BOTH COMPUTERS DOWN sign on the Black Hole door. Then he went in and started hustling around, plugging his ThinkPad pigtail into the phone line to see if he had e-mail, checking to see that his formula was stored on the computers. I can read part of his mind, and he was worried about The Watcher.

He was keeping busy, but then he froze.

"Listen," he whispered.

"What?"

"I said listen." He was definitely jumpy.

I didn't hear anything. Aaron pointed to the closed door and put a finger to his lips. I still didn't hear anything. But I was right by the door, so I jerked it open.

Fishface Pierrepont fell in. He spun around to leave, but I closed the door. I probably looked reasonably big to him. Next to Aaron, he's the shortest kid in our grade, and the scrawniest.

"I just wanted to play some SimCity," he squawked.

"Fishface, can't you read?" Aaron's hands were on his hips. "Both computers are down."

"Give me a break," Fishface said. "You put that sign up yourself. It's common knowledge. You think you own the computer room. Anyway, Mrs. Newbery said I could."

"Mrs. Newbery's at the American Library Association national convention as we speak," Aaron snapped. "She didn't tell you squat."

Now Fishface and Aaron were nose to nose. In a way, it was funny. "Oh yeah?" they were snarling at each other. "Oh yeah?"

"Get out of here before I lose my temper," Aaron said.

Fishface left.

Aaron was really hot under the collar. I personally thought he was overreacting. "Aaron, if you're starting to suspect Fishface of being The Watcher, you're going to have to suspect everybody on the Upper East Side."

"I do." Now Aaron was snapping at me.

I got him out of there. He needed some air. I needed lunch. We went to the deli, where he could graze the takeout salad bar and I could grab a BLT-double-mayo-to-go. We went to do lunch on our rock in the park. We wandered around. Before you knew it, it was time to report for dog duty. As Aaron said, being hung up between Mr. Thaw and Miss Mather set up a real matrix.

We were a couple of minutes late, and Miss Mather was looking at her watch when she opened the door. Nanky-Poo's topknot just cleared the carrier bag as she was handed over. Aaron was still carrying his ThinkPad, so I had to carry her.

"Don't let her jump out into traffic," he said as we crossed Fifth Avenue. "Having to bring her back to Miss Mather three feet long and an inch thick with tread marks is all we need."

We made it to a little grassy spot in the park. Nanky-Poo peeled out of her carrier bag. She knew we were stuck with her, so she went sniffing around, taking her time. We dropped down for some sun, and Aaron flipped open his ThinkPad.

"Aaron, give it a rest."

"I'm just trying to reconstruct whatever I entered that put Nanky-Poo in my lap and sent Miss Mather back to—"

"Aaron, whatever your formula did has stuck us with dog duty for the foreseeable—"

"But last night was a giant leap forward."

"I thought it was 1942. That's a giant leap backward."

"In this case, backward is forward."

I kept an eye on Nanky-Poo in case she got ideas about wandering off.

"We're seeing a clear pattern here," Aaron said. "First Ophelia and Heather, then you and me. Now Nanky-Poo and Miss Mather. Get it?"

"No."

"It's a two-for-one deal every time. My formula's still cuckoo, but one thing's certain. As things stand now, it takes the Emotional Component of two people to line up with my numbers."

"Some of those people are dogs," I pointed out.

"Whatever."

"But then why did Nanky-Poo come up to the penthouse while Miss Mather went back in time?"

"That's basic," Aaron said. "That's like fifth grade. You can figure that."

I gave it a shot. "You mean that Nanky-Poo cellular-reorganized up to your microprocessors because when Miss Mather went back to 1942, it was before Nanky-Poo existed? Like Nanky-Poo was running for her life?"

"Bingo," Aaron said, pointing at my brain. "Of course, she'd probably have been okay curled up in a quiet corner, but she panicked.

"Miss Mather was running for her life too, in a way. And it really booted up her Emotional Component. My formula could have picked up her signal a mile away. Her biggest wish in life is to go back to that night in 1942."

"But she told her boyfriend that it wasn't how she wanted to remember that moment. Why go back?"

"Because it's the one evening of her life she'd like to change. It was a now-or-never moment. She never got married. Maybe her boyfriend never came back from the war."

Dusty New York sun filtered down through the trees. You could hear Fifth Avenue traffic in the distance, but nothing else.

"Like he died?"

"Could be. Maybe we could find out. It was World War II. We could work it into a project for History class. Thaw's going to make us do oral reports. You know how he thinks."

"Aaron, do we like it when The Watcher noses in on us? Let's keep out of other people's business. Especially adults. Besides, what could we do? You can't change history. Can you?"

"Mathematically, no," Aaron said.

But you could see his mind was working.

When Nanky-Poo did her business, he snapped on a plastic glove and reached for a Baggie. Then Nanky-Poo came over to me, stamped a paw in the grass, bulged her eyes at me, and whined.

"Check in the carrier bag for doggie candy," Aaron said.

I found a couple of pieces and handed them over to her. It doesn't take a dog long to train you.

When we got off the elevator on eleven, Miss Mather's door was already opening. I wanted to make a quick dog drop and get out of there. We were *this close* to freedom when she said, "You may come in and pay a call."

This looked like part of our punishment, so we filed in. The curtains in the living room were closed, so it was dim in there. The air hung dead in the room. Miss Mather nodded to two chairs, and she and Nanky-Poo settled on the sofa. It was amazing how much alike they looked. On a low table there were three cups, a teapot, and a plate of vanilla wafers.

"I expect you like it sweet." Miss Mather poured out a couple of steaming cups of tea. "You may have a cookie each. Nanky-Poo too, naturally." Nanky-Poo sat next to Miss Mather, still as a statue, waiting. "Teatime calls for conversation," Miss Mather added.

We didn't have any conversation, so Miss Mather said, "Excellent though my family pedigree is, Nanky-

Poo's is better. As you will not know the history of the shih tzu, I will tell you. They were temple dogs in ancient Tibet."

She broke off a piece of cookie, and it disappeared into Nanky-Poo. "The lamas believed that the noble shih tzu had the soul of a lion."

Nanky-Poo roared low in her throat for more cookie parts.

"They are not Chinese dogs—never think it. Only ignorant people assume they are cousins of the Pekinese."

Nanky-Poo gave a definite sneer.

"However, the Dowager Empress of China was a great breeder. The Chinese grew so fond of the shih tzu that they allowed none of them out of the country. When foreigners tried to take them away, the Chinese fed the dogs ground glass so they would die on the voyage."

Nanky-Poo swallowed.

"It was Lady Brownrigg who succeeded in introducing the breed to the western world. She was General Brownrigg's wife, you know, and a great friend of Papa's."

Aaron caught my eye and tapped his forehead. His lips formed one silent word: cuckoo.

"Nanky-Poo is best of breed, as you see," Miss Mather said. "Notice how well-feathered her paws are. And she has the face of a chrysanthemum."

Nanky-Poo posed.

Miss Mather fed her the rest of her cookie. "I have

always thought the shih tzu the most beautiful of animals."

She would.

It got quiet then. I couldn't drink anything this hot any faster.

"You are Huckley boys, I believe?"

We nodded.

"My older brother, Clarence 'Cotton' Mather, went to Huckley. All our brothers did. The standards of that school have fallen badly over the years. I was a Pence girl, you know."

"My sister goes to Pence," I said.

"I had thought she was expelled," Miss Mather said. "I have not seen her in her uniform lately."

"For the last month of school they could wear whatever they wanted to."

"I am sorry to hear it." Miss Mather pursed her old lips. "Young girls have no taste. And you are in summer school? You jumped on my head only early this morning."

I nodded.

"We're studying World War II in History." Aaron gave me a look.

Miss Mather stirred. "World War II as history? Fiddlesticks. The Punic Wars are history. The Battle of Waterloo is history. Bull Run is history. World War II is a current event. Who on earth is teaching you this recent occurrence as if it were history?"

"Mr. L. T. Thaw," we said.

Miss Mather gazed off into the distance. Then finally

she said, "Education is wasted on the young anyway. How I wish I were back in my plaid skirt at P—"

Aaron's cup clattered on the table. "Miss Mather, don't!" He was half out of his chair, waving a small hand in her face. "Don't wish for anything!"

She blinked, then stared. "Whyever not?"

He reached down for his ThinkPad. "I've got my formula stored in here for extra backup. It could interactivate with your wish."

Miss Mather was still staring. "And then what would happen?"

"You might get it."

She gave Aaron a really interested look. "And to think," she said, "*I* am considered eccentric."

I was amazed that Aaron told her. There are things you just don't talk about around adults. But then Miss Mather wasn't your regular adult.

"Is that device of yours on? It isn't recording our conversation, is it, or doing anything rude?"

"It isn't on," Aaron said, "but you never know. I've got a virus in my formula."

Miss Mather gave him a long look. You couldn't tell if she believed him or not. "Ah, childhood," she said finally. "My favorite storybooks were always about granting three wishes. And the moral of the story was that you must be careful what you wish for because you might get it. Will that appliance of yours grant three wishes?" She seemed to smile.

"It already has," Aaron said. "One of them was y—"

"In my day, we had storybooks," she said in a far-away voice. "Now you have machines." She crooked a finger at the ThinkPad. "And are such devices as that going to change us all?"

Aaron nodded. "We're talking cyberrevolution here. We're talking emerging technologies and totally new windows of opportunity. We're—"

"Fiddlesticks." Miss Mather sat back. "People never change. All the wishes of the young are about the future. All the wishes of the old are about the past. At least those have been the directions of my dreams."

The clock on her mantel struck five, and Miss Mather stood up.

"Tomorrow at four on the dot," she said. "We will not take tea every day. Only on occasion."

Then we were out of there, hearing the locks on her door clicking shut. Aaron was duck-walking down to the elevator. "She might not be," he mumbled. "It's possible she's not."

"Not what?"

"Not cuckoo," he said. "But she's lonesome."

14

Doodlebug Summer

Summer school droned on, and so did Mr. Thaw. We were up to here with World War II. He'd already divided us into teams for oral reports:

The Pacific Theater of Operations
Winning the Battle of the Atlantic Against the U-Boats
India and the Burma Road
Against Rommel in North Africa
etc.

Fishface Pierrepont had put up his hand that day. "I'm a pacificist," Fishface said, "a conscientious objector. I believe in peace at any price."

No wonder, since he's the second-smallest kid in class.

Mr. Thaw shot him a craggy look. "Pierrepont, a

conscientious objector could be jailed during World War II."

"Lock me up!" Fishface said in his screechy voice.

So he was assigned "The War on the Homefront," but the rest of us got shipped out to overseas posts. Aaron and I were "Victory in Europe: The Crucial Final Months."

"Zimmer and Lewis!" said Mr. Thaw, drawing a bead on us. "For your own good, make your report the best in the class. I myself lost a toe to frostbite during the Battle of the Bulge in the winter of forty-four. I will know whereof you speak."

Just our luck.

At least summer school's out early. Most afternoons we'd swing past the deli, then head for our rock until it was time to report to Miss Mather. Aaron always had his ThinkPad, of course. He was storing Victory in Europe data he'd accessed. Or so he said. He'd sit hunched on the rock like a gnome, forking up salad and squinting at his screen.

I'd doze off. Sometimes just before my eyelids drooped shut, I'd think I caught a glimpse of somebody snooping on us from behind a tree. I'd think it was The Watcher, but it probably wasn't. Also, if I went completely to sleep, I'd start seeing my closet door opening again right here in Central Park. One time I said to Aaron, "Think you could access some information on The Watcher?" just to hear what he'd say. But his mind was in orbit. He heard me with only one brain cell.

"When you hacked into the Big P—"

"Just shut up about that," he said.

"That could have given them a Code Red alert, and now maybe we're being stalked by the C.I.A. Maybe a rogue C.I.A. agent gone freelance. They're always firing people."

Aaron's hands hung over the keyboard. I was really distracting him. "Did that e-mail message sound like the C.I.A.?" he said. "That business about polymorphing our miserable small bodies? Please."

"Maybe a foreign power," I said, "but I still think it could be Daryl."

"Daryl's not that subtle," Aaron said. "When he's got a message for you, he grabs you by the back of the neck."

"Aaron, aren't you worried about The Watcher at all? He knows what we're up to. He—"

"Of course I'm worried about The Watcher." He shook two small fists in the air. "I was *born* worried. But right now I'm a whole lot more worried about packaging enough data for our History report to keep Thaw off our cases. Especially mine. And you're no help."

He had a point there. Basically I was leaving the research part of our report to him. All I knew about World War II for sure was that after the Battle of the Bulge, Mr. Thaw only had nine toes.

Then one afternoon when we reported for dog duty, Miss Mather didn't answer her door when we rang. We kept ringing, and Nanky-Poo seemed to be hurling herself against the other side of the door, wanting her walkies.

Aaron tried the knob, and the door opened. We stepped into the shadowy front hall. Nanky-Poo can jump as high as our waists when she really wants to go out. She was all over us.

"Miss Mather?" we said, but the apartment didn't answer.

"Maybe we can just take Nanky-Poo and leave," I muttered. But oh no, not Aaron. He eased into the living room, so I followed.

"Aaron, you weren't fiddling your formula on your ThinkPad this afternoon, were you?"

But the TV set was there. A *Wall Street Journal* was tucked into the arm of the sofa. Aaron went over and put his finger on the date. It was today's.

"The basic layout of this apartment is like yours, isn't it?" he said in a low voice. "Three bedroom, three and a half bath, den?"

"Aaron, let's not search the place. What if we went into the bathroom and Miss Mather was taking a bath or something. That wouldn't be good."

But now we were walking down a hall. The first bedroom was a dusty spare with nothing personal in it. We crept on. The next bedroom was different. A thin line of sunlight came in under a blind. I jumped a foot. I thought we'd been cellular-reorganized for sure. The room wasn't from our time.

But Aaron put up a finger. "No, it's now, sort of."

But it smelled old. On a chest of drawers everything was laid out like a man had just walked in from some other decade and emptied his pockets: penknife, gold toothpick, fountain pen, pocket watch on a long chain, a few buffalo nickels, and a money clip with a two-dollar bill. A schedule of Brooklyn Dodgers games for the 1949 season.

We looked up at the foggy mirror, and we both jumped. There he was.

We spun around, and it was his portrait hanging over the bed. Heavy brows, piercing eyes, plenty of chins, and a tall white collar.

"It's her papa," Aaron whispered. "It's Old Man Mather. She's made his room into a shrine."

Then we saw that the bed was turned down, and beside it his nightshirt was laid out across a chair. My flesh crept.

"Aaron, let's get out. He's probably been dead since the Dodgers were at Ebbets Field." Nanky-Poo herself wouldn't come into this room. She stood in the door with her head hanging down.

We crept out, and there was only one bedroom left.

The door was half open with a strong whiff of mothballs coming out. You could see part of the room with some dim sunlight slanting in. Above Miss Mather's bed was a picture of herself, probably. It was a little girl sitting with one leg tucked under on a bench. In her hair was a bow bigger than her head. She looked about six and serious.

"She's gone out. Let's take Nanky-Poo to the park." But why was I whispering? Aaron ambled into the room, so I did too.

"Ah, there you two are," Miss Mather said.

It almost gave me a heart attack. Aaron and I ran into each other's arms. Nanky-Poo waddled over to her.

Miss Mather was behind us by an old dresser. She was wearing some kind of costume, really out-of-date, like dress code. A gray-green tweedy suit with a badge, a dark-red sweater, and a strange old felt hat with a ripply brim and another badge on it. You couldn't tell who she was supposed to be.

"Notice that I still fit into my uniform." She posed a little.

My heart was still in my mouth, but Aaron said, "And what uniform would that be?"

"The W.V.S., of course. The Women's Voluntary Services. I had it laid away in mothballs in case it might come in handy again. And so it has."

She gave us some time to figure out for ourselves how it was coming in handy again. Then she gave up and said, "For your oral report in that so-called History class."

We'd told her we had to do a Victory in Europe oral report, and it had to be good because Mr. Thaw was on our case. We'd been to tea with her two or three times. We didn't mind it after a while, though I was personally up to here with vanilla wafers.

"You were in World War II?" Aaron gave her an owl look. "On our side?"

"Of course I was in World War II. Did you imagine I would sit at home while the world caught fire? And women won that war. If it had been left to the men, we'd still be in bomb shelters."

Aaron stroked his jaw. "That uniform doesn't look too American."

"It is the British W.V.S.," she said. "I crossed the Atlantic on a destroyer chased by U-boats in order to join. I am not British, of course, but the founder of the W.V.S. was the Marchioness of Reading, a great friend of Papa's."

Aaron looked thoughtful. "Your papa let you join up in the war?"

"He was a great patriot," she said. Then she looked out to the hall and across at his room. "And I suppose he would rather have seen me dead than married."

Silence fell, and you could see these little nebulas of dust dots in the slanting sunshine.

"I have a scrapbook of my wartime career," she said, dragging it out of a dresser drawer. "You will be interested in it. It will be invaluable for your report."

In her uniform she moved like a young girl. She dropped down on the end of her bed and motioned Aaron and me to sit with her. Nanky-Poo jumped up to join us, thinking this was teatime.

"What did you do?" I asked.

"Whatever I was assigned to do," Miss Mather said. "I developed a talent for driving staff cars and ambulances during air raids. Women are better drivers than men, you know. Men are too easily distracted. The Blitz was long over before I reached Europe, and so London had already been thoroughly bombed. But then in the summer of forty-four, the Nazis sent over their secret weapon."

"The doodlebug," Aaron said.

Miss Mather had opened to a scrapbook page that was snapshots of bomb craters. "So you know about the doodlebug." She turned to me. "It was the flying bomb that could come over anytime, day or night."

Aaron nodded. "I've got doodlebug data stored in my Inline Memory Module."

"So do I," Miss Mather said in a long-ago voice.

She talked us through the scrapbook of her doodlebug summer until the room began to get shadowy. The book was full of black-and-white snapshots: Miss Mather working under the hood of her ambulance, Miss Mather on parade in her dress uniform, Miss Mather in a London park, drinking tea in her metal helmet. "This is my gas mask carrier, not a purse," she said, pointing it out. "We never knew what Hitler would send us next."

I wanted to ask her about Teddy, but I didn't know how. I wondered if she'd joined up in the war so she could find him. He wasn't in her scrapbook.

Then Aaron said, "What happened to your boyfriend?"

The room dimmed a little more.

"I had several," she said softly, "naturally."

"Did they all come back?"

"Not to me." She closed the book.

She stood up, and it was time for us to go to the park. Somehow I wasn't in a big hurry to leave, though Nanky-Poo was beginning to get desperate. She was out at the front door, hurling herself against it again.

"I'd like to get you on tape for our report," Aaron

said. "With your data, Miss Mather, we'll be a shoo-in for an A each. You'd be like oral history—I mean oral current event."

"Certainly not," she said, showing us out. "I do not speak to machines. Besides, it won't be necessary."

Whatever that meant.

I dreamed that night. It wasn't about The Watcher. It was even realer than that.

Aaron was in it, and he looked ridiculous. He was in dress code, but it sure wasn't Huckley's: boxy little striped jacket, flannel shorts with his knobby knees showing, long socks, a little cap with a bill on his head. Hilarious. I looked down, and I was wearing the same. We were British schoolboys, with gas masks.

I looked around, and we were in a crowd of other British schoolboys, outdoors somewhere. I looked up into a gray sky, and I thought it was full of Fuji Film blimps. But they were barrage balloons sent up on cables to try to keep the Nazis from dive-bombing. Somehow I knew we were outside a railroad station. You couldn't tell. Every wall was sandbagged. We were waiting for a train to take us all out of London, away from danger. We were being evacuated.

Then we heard an eerie sound—a distant *putt-putt*ing high up. People began to duck. There it was, a small black sliver shape, like a needle in the sky, sewing the clouds. It angled in, *putt-putt*ing louder, with a flame in its tail. My heart was in my mouth. It looked like home-delivery death.

A khaki-colored ambulance with blacked-out headlights pulled up at the curb, and Miss Mather jumped out. It was the young Miss Mather in her W.V.S. uniform.

We all stood like statues, watching the doodlebug bomb get bigger. Its engine quit. The *putt-putt*ing stopped cold. That meant the bomb had reached its destination. It was falling now, on our heads.

Miss Mather made a run for us. She could run like a deer. She had us all inside, somehow, at the last moment. We were in the echoing station, and the bomb fell somewhere just outside. A thump you felt in your stomach sucked all the air out of the world.

We were sprawled on a floor, just barely safe. Glass rained. There was grit in my mouth from the sandbags. If this was a dream, it was a real production.

I struggled to sit up, and I was sweating buckets. The sun was coming in the window of my room. It was a school day.

15

Three More Wishes

Later Aaron said it was fate that drew us back to the Black Hole that afternoon.

We were into oral reports in History. Zach Zeckendorf and Pug Ulrich were being chased all over North Africa by Rommel. Then Mr. Thaw would horn in to tell us where they got their facts wrong. Our own report was just a question of time, and we were getting down to the wire. After school when we were buying lunch at the deli, Aaron said we'd better go back to the Black Hole to work. He was having trouble seeing his ThinkPad screen in the glaring sun of the park.

If it had been an overcast day, we'd have gone to the park. Fate.

The halls at school had emptied out. Aaron handed me his salad and Snapple and dug for his key. But the media center was unlocked. We went in through the book area. Aaron's hand was on the knob of the Black Hole door when he froze.

He put up a finger. "The computers are booted up," he whispered. Nothing wrong with his hearing. We listened.

A voice from inside the Black Hole said, "Plastic or cash. I don't take IOU's." A somewhat familiar voice.

"Okay, stand right there," the voice said to somebody in the Black Hole, "and really concentrate."

We didn't breathe.

Then we heard a click and a sizzle. The door vibrated. We burst in.

Formula—it looked like Aaron's formula—was displayed on both screens. Somebody sat hunched between them. He spun around. Fishface Pierrepont.

Aaron lunged. He was going for Fishface's throat, and my hands were full of lunch. The Snapples jumped out of my hands. Salad went everywhere.

I had Aaron in a hammerlock. Fishface was clutching both sides of his own head. He had terror written all over him. Also guilt.

"Fishface!" I said. *"You're The Watcher."*

Aaron was trying to be calm. I eased up on him. "What's this?" he said in a dangerous voice. He was pointing to a pile of money on the table. Reasonably big money. There was a fifty-dollar bill. Aaron picked up a major credit card. I read it over his shoulder. It belonged to Dud Dupont.

Fishface was plastered against the screens, dreaming

of escape. In the voice of a mouse he squeaked, "I was just playing some Sim—"

Aaron started to lunge again, but I held him back. Rage rippled through him, but he said, "Let go of me, Josh."

Fishface's desperate eyes were on the door.

"You're not going anywhere," Aaron said, nose to nose with him. "Talk. You've been hacking. You've been snooping. You've been all over us. You've called up my formula, and you're a cybernetic illiterate. You don't know a hologram from a hole in the ground. You don't—"

"You think you're the only one who knows anything." Fishface was a trapped rat with a mouse voice. "Your formula was stone age. I upgraded it. I zeroized and reexpressed some of your cockamamie mathematics."

Cords stood out in Aaron's neck. "What's this money about? Where's Dud Dupont?"

"In cyberspace," Fishface said, and stuck out his lower lip.

We stood there. Fishface could be bragging. He made a quick move.

"Don't even think about it," Aaron said. "Make my day."

I couldn't believe it, but Fishface had turned Aaron's formula into a business—like a travel agency, for Pete's sake. He was charging people for trips to cyberspace.

The full horror of it hit us. Aaron smacked his own forehead. "Fishface, how long have you been doing this?"

"Just today," he muttered. "This was like my grand opening."

"Fishface, how many? Who's involved here? Tell me it's just Dud Dupont."

"It is," Fishface said, "plus Wimp Astor and Pug Ulrich."

"No." Aaron's face dropped into his hands. "No, no, no, no. You mean you just moved them out—boom, boom, boom?"

"I told you I improved your formula," Fishface said with quiet pride. "I made them pay, and I sent them away." He even had his own advertising jingle.

Aaron grabbed the air. "But money won't do it. It takes Emotional Component to interact with the formula. They really have to *want* to go."

"They did. I told them to want to go someplace, and they went," Fishface said. "They're rich guys. They always get what they want."

We reeled.

"Get out of the way." Aaron swept Fishface aside and settled at the screens. His hands hovered over the keyboards.

"They have to come back on their own," Fishface said, "like you guys did when you seniorized. That's basic."

"Shut up, Fishface," Aaron moaned. "My formula was already virused. Who knows how it operates now that you've hacked it around? Who knows if they're *ever* coming back?"

He signed off and sat round-shouldered in front of the dead screens. Silence fell. Time stood still.

"We better stay here," I said, "in case they—"

Aaron shook his head. "It's like the watched pot. It never boils. And why do I have the feeling they're not coming back here?"

He turned around to glare at Fishface like he still wanted to pop him right in the retainer. "This is totally your fault. If there's a rap to take, you'll take it. If Pug and Wimp and Dud are gone for good, we're talking network news here. We're talking national manhunt. We're talking lawsuits and court dates and adult involvement. We're talking *Hard Copy*. And all because you messed with something way over your head."

"Like you didn't," Fishface sneered. Quicker than the eye, he swept up the money and Dud's credit card.

He nearly made it to the door when Aaron said, "Freeze."

Fishface did, and Aaron said, "Just keep your distance, Fishface. If we have anything to say to each other, it'll be fax to fax. I've got a little jingle for you: *Stay off our cases and out of our faces.*"

Fishface fled.

The next day Pug Ulrich, Wimp Astor, and Dud Dupont weren't in History. They were Absent Without Leave the rest of the week. Fishface was there every day, of course, with his hands clasped on his desktop like a choirboy—perfect attendance. Aaron would stumble into class pink-eyed and green-faced. He was piping in CNN on one of his home screens all night, listening for this news to break internationally. He was calling me up every evening.

"Look, if we could just figure out where they wanted to go, we could try cellular-reorganizing ourselves and go find—"

"What we?"

"But they've probably gone in three different directions anyway. Who knows? With whatever Fishface has done to my formula, they could all three end up as a dinosaur's dinner."

I was pretty worried too. For one thing, we hadn't been gone this long when we'd cyberspaced ourselves. Also, I had a bad feeling we'd end up getting busted for this. Don't we always?

It was a long week followed by an endless weekend. I basically walked through it. On Monday Aaron and I got to History early. We'd been coming in early every day, hoping against hope. Aaron slumped into class, dragging his ThinkPad. He'd lost some weight.

And there they were.

Pug. Wimp. Dud. They were swaggering around as usual, except they all had great tans. Pug was beginning to peel. Fishface was at his desk, smiling quietly into his clasped hands.

My knees buckled with relief.

Aaron zeroed right in on Pug. "Okay, let's hear about it. Where you been?"

"Since when are you taking attendance?" Pug said. Pug's pretty pompous, and Aaron and I aren't exactly in his peer group. "Provence, if it's any of your business," Pug said, "the south of France."

"I know where Provence is," Aaron snapped. "Go on."

"My parents have a country house there for the summers. I dropped in. Flew back last night on Air France. First class, of course."

But Aaron was already moving on to Wimp. "Talk to me, Wimp."

Wimp blinked. His name tells it all. He's the third-shortest kid in class. He and Aaron were eye to eye. "Martha's Vineyard. It's an island off Cape Cod."

"I know it's an island off Cape Cod," Aaron said.

"Actually, my parents own most of it," Wimp remarked. "I grabbed a commuter flight back."

But now Aaron was bearing down on Dud. "Tell me about it, Dud."

"Santorini. It's a Greek isle. My parents have a villa there. Fishface sent me over, and I flew back on the Concorde. Fishface is a genius."

Aaron's mouth opened and closed.

He wandered back to my desk, half relieved, half disgusted. "Well, anyway, they're back. They weren't even missing. They were with their *parents*, for Pete's sake. And they made lateral moves." He dropped his ThinkPad on my desk and propped it open. "Let me just make a note of that."

"They took *vacations*?" I smacked my forehead.

"What are they going to want next, *frequent-flyer miles*?"

He waved a small hand. The classroom was in its usual uproar, but he lowered his voice. "Not vacations. They're rich kids. Their parents are never around. Their parents are always on yachts or something, keeping their distance. In a way, it's a little bit sad. They got what they most wanted—a little time with their families. They got their wishes."

Three wishes.

"So it takes the Emotional Component of two *or more*," Aaron said. "Let me make a note of that."

"Aaron, they've all got big mouths. What if they tell on us?"

"What us? They're giving Fishface all the credit." Aaron rolled his eyes. "Anyway, if you're talking about adults, who'd believe them?"

I closed his ThinkPad lid for him. "Aaron, let's call it quits right now. Let's not—"

"You kidding me?" He was already gearing back up. "Most of the great discoveries of science are accidental. I've got my original formula stored here in the ThinkPad and at home on my technopolis. We've got Fishface's version on the Black Hole terminals. Once I get the two synthesized, we're talking—"

But Mr. Thaw suddenly invaded the classroom. "MAN YOUR BATTLE STATIONS," he roared, and everybody fell into the nearest seat.

Mr. Thaw scanned us from the front of the room. Nothing wrong with his eyesight.

"Ah, nice of you to drop in, Dupont, Astor, Ulrich." His old voice dripped with sarcasm, but what was he going to do to them? Pug had already given his North Africa report, so he was half off the hook. Dud's grandmother left Huckley School four million and change in her will. And Wimp is an Astor. These aren't deserters you shoot.

But Mr. Thaw was still scanning the room. Then he spotted us, though I was as far down in my seat as I could get. I was practically sitting on the back of my neck.

"Zimmer. Lewis. According to my battle plan, this is the day for your oral report. 'Victory in Europe: The Crucial Final Months,' I believe? You may begin at once. Bring up your heavy artillery."

"No." Aaron's head hit his desk. "No, no, no, no."

16
Victory in Europe

I panicked. How could we be thinking oral reports with all we'd had on our minds? School should come later in life, when you can concentrate better.

Aaron climbed out of his seat, looking older than Mr. Thaw. We didn't have a note between us, and Aaron couldn't take his ThinkPad with him. You can figure for yourself what Mr. Thaw thought about ThinkPads.

"You too, Lewis," he said, nailing me. "Out of your foxhole and up here on the front line."

Aaron trudged up the aisle. I followed, my head whirling. Maybe I could talk about that dream of mine when we were British schoolboys being evacuated. . . . Maybe I could ask Mr. Thaw to take off his shoe and sock and show us his missing toe from the Battle of the Bulge. He might be willing. Maybe I could . . .

Then we were at the front of the room with every eye on us. Fishface smiled quietly. Behind us Mr. Thaw was propped against the blackboard, ready to pounce on our first factual error. You could feel him back there, hear him breathing.

"Picture it," Aaron said in a wobbly voice. "The crucial final summer of the war dawning on a battle-weary Europe. Italy in—er—Allied hands at last. France—ah —crying out for liberation. While in England massive multinational forces gathered for the . . . important invasion of Normandy."

"Important, to say the least," Mr. Thaw grumbled behind us.

Go, Aaron, I thought. Keep it rolling. Fill the whole class period. But he wasn't having one of his better days. He was reaching for every word. Boy, did I wish I could reorganize my cells out of there. If Emotional Component alone would do it, I'd be on Mars.

". . . England, brought low by—let's see—five years of war, was the great staging area for the D-day invasion of . . . like, June sixth . . ."

"When suddenly a crazed and desperate Hitler, his unspeakable empire crumbling around his ears, launched the last and most demoralizing weapon of an inhumane war."

Except Aaron didn't say those last words.

Somebody else did. It was a lady's voice from the door. She was standing on the threshold, and she was quite an unusual sight. An old lady in complete Women's Voluntary Services uniform, along with cotton stockings, ripply hat, and a gas mask container hanging from her shoulder.

Miss Mather.

For some reason she was carrying a monkey wrench and a tire iron.

She strode into the classroom on squeaky shoes. Everybody blinked. "What's this?" somebody said. "Virtual reality?" Behind us Mr. Thaw wasn't breathing.

" 'Doodlebugs' and 'buzz bombs' the British public called these pilotless payloads raining sudden death upon the London landscape," Miss Mather proclaimed, "an early example of the ramjet engine in unfortunate action. The Nazis launched them by day and by night from their infernal installation in the Pas de Calais, and now the embattled Britons must endure one final challenge on their long road to victory!"

Miss Mather had remembered when our oral report was due, even if we hadn't. Aaron's eyes were bulging at her like Nanky-Poo's. Relief was breaking over his brow. It was like she'd stepped right out of World War II to tell us all about it.

It looked like we'd planned her as our oral report all along.

"It was women, naturally enough, who won the war. Women on the assembly line." Miss Mather waved her wrench. "Women behind the wheels of a thousand careening ambulances." She waved her tire iron. "Women stitching up the fabric of a torn civilization!"

She had us all in the palm of her hand even before she hit Omaha Beach for us. We were all there with her as she liberated Paris. By now a few people at the back of the classroom were up on their desks, yelling, "On to Berlin!"

Finally she wound down in the exact last minute of class. By then her old voice was young.

She'd done our oral report. Then she turned our way.

But her old eyes skated past us. Her wrench and her tire iron hit the floor as she opened her arms to Mr. Thaw.

"Hello, Teddy," she said to him.

17

Just a Few Flowers,
Just a Few Friends

Mr. Thaw often said, "Contrary to popular opinion, it is perfectly possible to flunk summer school." But nobody did. I got a B. Aaron got a B plus.

After the day Miss Mather did our oral report, she said we didn't have to report for dog duty anymore. We were like out on parole, but we were always welcome to drop by for teatime.

Once school was over, it looked like we had summer pretty well wrapped up. I was basically hoping that nothing more would happen. Something did.

August is New York's stickiest month, and the smart money's out of town. But even on the hottest days Mom walked home from Barnes Ogleby in her business suit and Adidas. She's something of a power walker. One afternoon she came home pretty much wiped out, and we made a pitcher of iced tea with mint. She was sprawled on the living room sofa, sipping, when the front doorbell rang.

"I'll get it!" Heather yelled from her room. It couldn't be Muffie, who was in the Hamptons and had seemed to forget she knew Heather. It couldn't be Stink, who actually *didn't* know her. But Heather was still living in hope. I kind of wondered if it might be the C.I.A.

Mom and I waited. Then Heather showed up in the doorway, looking confused. Her eyes were big and blinky. She was forming silent words with her mouth: *It's . . . her.* Heather pointed to the floor. *It's the old bat from down—*

"Thank you, my dear," Miss Mather said, stepping into the doorway. Same old Miss Mather, except there was something different about it. Of course she wasn't wearing her W.V.S. uniform, not in this weather. But there was something else. She'd painted all her nails with red polish.

The iced-tea glass hung in Mom's hand.

"Ah, Josh," Miss Mather said, peering into the living room. "How nice to see you. Nanky-Poo sends her regards."

Mom nudged me, and I stood up. Miss Mather came forth. "Mrs. Lewis, I have been remiss about paying calls and not nearly as neighborly as I should have been."

We'd lived here on top of her since I was preschool. Mom's eyes were huge. ". . . Tea?" she said.

Miss Mather smiled.

I went out to the kitchen for another glass. We didn't have vanilla wafers, but I found some Oreos. When I got back, Miss Mather was sitting on the sofa next to Mom where I'd been.

"I was myself a Pence girl, you know." She leaned nearer Mom. "They show improvement later on."

Heather was still in the doorway, amazed.

"Thank you, Josh." Miss Mather took the glass in her little red-tipped claw. "You may sit over there." She pointed me into a chair and turned back to Mom. "Such a well-mannered boy. He does you proud. I do enjoy the calls he pays on me with his little friend."

Mom's head revolved slowly between Miss Mather and me. I hadn't ever happened to mention to her about dog duty.

"Josh?" she said faintly. "Calls?"

"Why yes." Miss Mather slapped one of her sharp little knees. "Josh is quite like a great-nephew to me. Of course I have always thought of you all as . . . extended family."

"Us?" Mom murmured.

"And so I wonder if I might ask a great favor."

You could have heard a pin drop.

"As I expect Josh has told you, I have recently rekindled an acquaintance with an old beau."

She meant Mr. Thaw.

"Beau?" Mom said. "Oh."

"It is all thanks to Josh and to his little friend that Teddy Thaw and I have been reunited. Fate and our own foolish pride had kept us apart." She laid a small paw on Mom's sleeve. "Though he little realized it, Josh played his part as Cupid."

From the doorway Heather made a strangled sound.

Mom edged up on the sofa. She'd already had a long day, and her mind was trying to process this data.

"That would be Mr. Thaw, the History teacher at Huckley, and . . . you, Miss Mather?"

"Call me Margaret," Miss Mather told Mom. "All my friends do. At least they did when they were alive. Teddy and I agree that we have lost quite enough time. More than fifty years, in fact." A faint color came over her face. She was blushing.

"Of course it will be just a small wedding at home. But as I have only a small number of blood relatives left, I wonder if you would all attend. And perhaps see to some of the arrangements. Just a few flowers, just a few friends."

In the doorway Heather stared.

After Miss Mather left, Mom gazed into her empty iced-tea glass. She was lost in thought, almost cyberspaced. "Josh, will I ever need to know why you and Aaron have been paying calls on Miss Mather?"

"I don't think so, Mom," I said. "With any luck, no."

You may have read about the wedding in *The New York Times*, the "Lifestyles" section:

Romance Interrupted by World War II
Proceeds Slightly Off Schedule

It was that last Saturday in August, the most humid day of the year. Miss Mather's living room was banked with flowers. Mom had rented an organ and hired a lady to play it. Quite a few people turned out, considering this was summer in the city. Several people from the apartment building came, including Mr. and Mrs. Zimmer. A small group of Huckley faculty members came, though Trip Renwick was still up at soccer camp. And some other people too. After all, as *The Times* said, the Mathers and the Thaws are among the oldest families in New York.

Dad came. My dad. He flew in from Chicago. He said he had to see this for himself. Hey, whatever it takes.

The aisle was just the middle of Miss Mather's living room. Heather went first, carrying a small basket of daisies. She'd given Mom a lot of grief about this.

"I'm supposed to start my career as a bridesmaid for an eighty-year-old bride? Mo-om." But she got a new, really mature dress out of it. And she secretly thought that bridesmaiding was basically a pretty grown-up job. She was thirteen by now, and it had really gone to her head.

"But I'll need three-inch heels to complete the look," Heather said. "I'm not negotiable about that."

Next down the aisle were Aaron and me in Huckley dress code. I was burning up in mine. He was carrying a cushion with the rings. I had Nanky-Poo on a leash. She waddled along with a new bow in her topknot. We looked ridiculous, and Heather's still calling me Cupid.

There by a portable altar waited Mr. L. T. Thaw. It

was like being in class. Beside him was his best man, the headmaster. They both had white carnations in their buttonholes, and Mr. Thaw's new groom suit was a dead ringer for all his old suits. If he could stand up straight, he'd be over six feet tall. The headmaster was a lot taller than that. They both really loomed. As Aaron and I approached, the headmaster's eyes narrowed at us. Nothing wrong with his memory.

Then came Mom. She was matron of honor. She had a new dress too and carried a bouquet. She looked really pretty, but there was something dazed in her eyes.

The organ music swelled, and Miss Mather appeared in her doorway. Mom had come down early to help her dress. She carried a load of lilies and wore her own mother's wedding gown. It practically had a bustle, but she didn't wear a veil. "At my time of life," she'd told Mom, "I think we can dispense with that." Her old eyes swept the room and found Mr. Thaw. He was looking craggily back. She blushed. He smiled. A first.

She came down the aisle on her own. You could hear the squeak of her regular shoes under her lacy skirts. Her papa was long gone, but she'd propped his picture on the mantel. He glared down at all of us. What he'd have thought of this wedding you wouldn't want to know.

So that was basically it. Miss Mather and Mr. Thaw were married. The ceremony was fairly short, conducted by the clergyperson from St. James church around the corner on Madison Avenue. Aaron handed up the rings to them, and they finally threw caution to the winds. They even kissed at the end like a regular bride and groom, and it wasn't a quickie either.

Then Mr. Thaw spoke a few words. Looking down at Miss Mather, who was still clasped in his arms, he said in a big classroom voice, "Margaret, I gaze upon your webbed beauty with an eye too old to wander farther afield. Whatever is left of me is yours."

The room stirred, and Mom made a strangled sound. But this is probably how teachers get married. Put them at the front of a room, and they have to have their say.

For the reception, Vince came up from the front door to pour the punch.

The best part of it was that Dad was there. He was looking good in his summer blazer. Then when it was time for pictures, we had a separate one taken of us Lewises as a family. It's still in a frame in our living room. Heather's on one side, clutching her daisy basket. I'm on the other, sweating buckets in my dress code. If you look close, Dad's hand is holding Mom's.

The whole event was almost too much for Mr. Thaw. He had to sit down to drink his punch. But Miss Mather—Mrs. Thaw—got him up to cut the cake. She bustled around, serving slices, introducing people, swooping in her old skirts.

Then she was leading this big, senior-size guy up to meet Heather. Heather looked up all six feet of him, and her daisies quivered.

"My dear," Mrs. Thaw said, "I wonder if you have met my great-nephew, Otis?"

I looked again, and my eyes popped. It was Otis

"Stink" Stuyvesant. I knew that. But I sure hadn't expected to see him here. I'd been hoping I'd never see him again anywhere. I grabbed Aaron by the arm. "Aaron, her great-nephew is Stink Stuyvesant," I blurted.

"As you say," Mrs. Thaw said. "We Mathers and the Stuyvesants have intermarried several times over several centuries."

Heather stared up at Stink, and you could see the whole roof of her mouth. She'd been waiting all summer for him to call, and here he was. Did she realize that he didn't look anything like the Stink she thought she'd met? No. I can read Heather's mind. You don't have to be a rocket scientist.

When she could breathe, Heather sighed, "I loved your letter."

Aaron and I were right there, under Stink's elbow— silent, listening.

Stink dug a big shoe toe modestly into the carpet. "Hey"—he shrugged—"I'm in it mostly for the exercise."

Aaron and I stared at each other. Stink thought that Heather meant his *athletic* letter. He'd lettered in both lacrosse and soccer.

But I doubt if Heather heard him. She couldn't wait to speed dial Muffie McInteer.

And there behind Stink was his own picture in a silver frame on the table next to the sofa where Mr. and Mrs. Thaw were sitting now, close together. Nanky-Poo too, thinking it was teatime.

147

When the reception was over, I sort of wished it wasn't. Then we Lewises were all in the elevator, heading home.

"You been behaving okay?" Dad said with a hand on my shoulder. "Not acting out?"

"Not lately, Dad," I said, "but I'm right on the edge. You better hang around. I could use some supervision."

"Maybe I will," he said, giving Mom a look. "And there's a little summer left. I've rented a house for Labor Day weekend. A little sun. A little swimming, maybe some tennis. Just the four of us. It's in the Hamptons."

Heather clutched her forehead. She was wearing a lot more eyeliner than Mom usually allows. "Da-ad," she said, "I couldn't possibly go to the Hamptons. All those same old faces? Like enough already. Besides, Stink's in town."

Aaron gave me a jingle that night, late. Same old Aaron.

"I've been doing some heavy-duty collating and really taking a hard look at my formula. Actually, Fishface did us a favor—the little insect. I've been synthesizing, and we're going to be able to go electronically with our every need and move ourselves out—boom, boom. Past, future, lateral moves. Foolproof. We're virtually there, Josh, with a byte-driven interactive dream machine vaccinated for viruses. We've got a command system here to cybernetically realize our every wish."

I was already beginning to pack for the Hamptons. "Aaron," I told him, "I've already got mine."

And at that very second the lights in my room went out. I could hear Aaron's strangled gasp.

"Aaron, don't tell me you're soldering. I don't want to hear that."

"You kidding?" he said. "Of course I'm not soldering. I'm talking to you. It's not me. Check out your window."

I did and the whole neighborhood was blacked out. This happens. It's a New York thing.

Now my phone was squawking in Aaron's voice. "My formula!" he squawked. "My formula! No, no, no, no, no."

He'd dropped the phone. You could hear him racing around the room, practically bouncing off the walls.

Back to the drawing board.

Richard Peck

is the acclaimed author of more than twenty novels
for young people, most recently *Lost in Cyberspace*
(Dial), the first book about Josh and Aaron's adven-
tures. Mr. Peck's other novels include *Ghosts I Have
Been*, an ALA Best of the Best Books for Young
Adults and a *New York Times* Outstanding Book of
the Year, and three other books in the popular Blossom Culp series; *Father Figure*, an ALA Best Book
for Young Adults, and *Voices After Midnight*.

   Mr. Peck has received several awards for the body
of his work: the 1990 Margaret A. Edwards Award
from *School Library Journal* and the ALA; the 1990
National Council of Teachers of English/ALAN
Award; and the 1991 Medallion from the University
of Southern Mississippi, honoring an author who has
made an outstanding contribution to the field of lit-
erature. He is also a two-time winner of the Edgar
Allan Poe Award for best juvenile mystery. He lives
in New York City.